Anna the Girl Witch 1

Foundling Witch

Vic Connor

illustrated by

Raquel Barros

Helvetic House

Second edition, expanded and rewritten.

Also by Vic Connor:
Tommy Hopps and the Aztecs
Max!
The Story Traveler

ISBN: 978-1-5202707-8-4

Contents

PART I:
INTO THE LABYRINTH

lab·y·rinth
noun

A complex and unusual maze
of passages or paths in
which it's difficult to reach the exit
or find one's way.

Chapter 1

ear Diary,

I've never written in a diary before, and I must say, it feels a little strange. I'm not even quite sure how to begin.

Should I first tell you some basic things about myself? Things like: My name is Anna Sophia Medvedeva. I live in a dormitory at the Collège du Parc Cézanne in Geneva, Switzerland, and my uncle Misha found me living in a cave with bears when I was just a few weeks old.

Or should I just start by writing thoughts about things that are important to me? Things like: I've been alive for exactly 4,749 days, and today is the best day of all.

Why? Because today is June 12th and it's my thirteenth birthday, and I'm officially a teenager!

Happy Birthday to me!

I'm so excited I feel like I'm bubbling up inside. I don't know why, but it just feels like something magical is going to happen today, and I can't wait to see what it is.

This diary is my birthday present to myself. I got the idea for it in history class after Sister Mary Agnes read to us from a diary written by a girl named Anne Frank. Her birthday was June 12th too, although she was born a long time ago in 1929. Her parents had given her a diary on her thirteenth birthday, so she'd have a private place to write down all her thoughts. For two years, while she and her family were in hiding from the Nazis during World War II, Anne did exactly that. I loved hearing her thoughts about herself and her family, and about the world. Someday, I hope I can read her whole book.

Well, that's all I can think of to say right now, Diary. After I see what the day brings, maybe I'll have something more exciting to tell you. For now, I'll just say, thanks for listening, and I'll talk to you later.

Signed,
Anna Sophia, teenager

Even though it wasn't quite six in the morning, I heard a rustling outside my door. I couldn't imagine anyone else being awake. Except for the nuns, no one in the orphanage woke up before 7:30 on a Saturday.

I crept toward the door in my bare feet and put my ear against it to listen. Someone was definitely out there.

I whipped the door open, and my friend Lauraleigh Jeanneret came stumbling into the room, nearly knocking me over as she recovered her balance. A giant sign fluttered to the floor.

"Oh. Wow!" Lauraleigh cried out. "Sorry, Anna Sophia. I was trying to surprise you with a happy birthday sign taped to your door." She looked slightly embarrassed when she added, "I thought you'd be asleep."

"Oh, gosh. I've been up for hours," I said happily. "I just couldn't sleep!"

Lauraleigh grinned. "That's because you're thirteen today. Even though it was five years ago, I remember feeling the same way when I became a teenager. It's a special birthday." She smiled at me, and for about the millionth time since I'd come to the Luyons Orphanage when I was six, I felt grateful for her friendship.

I like all the kids who live at both the Luyons Orphanage and Collège du Parc Cézanne right next door to it, but Lauraleigh is special. It's like she's my real sister, the way she knows what I'm thinking the second it pops into my mind. Even though we're not related by blood, I honestly think of her as part of my family.

It's like that with Uncle Misha, too. I couldn't possibly love him any more than I do now, even if he was a real blood uncle.

Uncle Misha is a trapper. I think he's a very good one, because every year when he comes from Siberia to see me, he brings his sable furs with him. Then he sends them all the way to New York City. In America. I don't think many Russian trappers sell their furs to companies in America.

Lauraleigh once told me a Russian sable coat could sell for as much as twenty thousand American dollars. I can't even imagine that much money! I'm not sure she was right, though, because if that were true, Uncle Misha would be rich. And he isn't — he lives all by himself in the middle of Siberia not far from Lake Baikal and makes all his clothes from the animals he traps and hunts. He almost never buys anything from a store.

Just thinking about Uncle Misha makes me miss him.

He's a great, big man with a bushy, black beard. He has black eyebrows he can wiggle, so they look like caterpillars crawling across his face. As a little girl, if I ever felt sad about something, he'd wiggle his eyebrows and ask if I knew where the caterpillars were going. It would make me laugh, and I'd forget all about whatever had made me unhappy.

People might not know it when they first see him, but Uncle Misha is in tune with the spirit world. It's how he found me. He said a spirit came to him in the night and told him to go to Mama Bear's den because I needed him.

"Now, you have to be a little daft to go into the den of a giant bear," he would say whenever I asked him to tell me the story. We called it the Anna Sophia Story; until I was six and sent away, I made him tell it a hundred times. "But that's exactly what I did!"

"Tell me again how you knew to go find me," I would say when I wanted to hear it again.

And he'd say, "Well... the spirit of a beautiful woman came to me in the night." He'd look at the ceiling and stroke his beard before continuing. "It was July first, and the only time in my memory that a blizzard occurred in July."

"A *little* blizzard?"

"Oh, no!" Uncle Misha would say, wiggling his eyebrows. "A huge blizzard. A blizzard so big you couldn't see a finger in front of your face, should you have been so foolish as to step outside."

"But how could you find me if you couldn't see?"

"Well, the spirit told me exactly where to go, and then she guided me all the way there."

"What did she look like?" I always asked, even though I knew the answer.

"Ahhh, well; spirits don't always have shapes or colors like we do," Uncle Misha would explain in a gentle voice. "But I can tell you; she carried the scent of an ancient pine tree standing in the forest on a summer's day. And when she spoke, her voice sounded like a babbling brook dancing and weaving its way over tiny pebbles made of glass. So, I think she must have been very beautiful."

"And she told you where to go?"

"Oh yes," Uncle Misha said. "She told me to look inside Mama Bear's den at the foot of Blind Wolf's Bluff."

"And you went there in the storm?" My eyes would be so wide open it was a wonder they didn't pop out.

"I did." He'd nod. "And do you know what I found?"

I already knew, but I'd shake my head anyway, eager to hear it again.

"I found a tiny baby all wrapped up in furs and nestled together with the other cubs. She was a little girl, only a few weeks old. And once I saw her, the spirit woman whispered in my ear. She told me the little baby had been born on the twelfth day of June, under a moon so full it lit up all the worlds; even the worlds human people can't see.

"'Her name is Anna Sophia,' the spirit whispered. And when she said those two words, *Anna Sophia*, it was as if your name floated through the air wrapped in the gossamer wings of angels."

Uncle Misha always sighed then, as if the memory of something so beautiful forced the air right out of his massive chest.

"And I was wrapped up, snuggled next to the bear cubs?" I'd ask.

"Yes, you were, *Malyshka*," Uncle Misha would answer, using the Russian endearment for *Little One*. "Mama Bear took care of you as if you were one of her own."

I'd always pause then as if the next question was one I wasn't sure I should ask. But I'd always ask it, anyway. "Was the spirit woman my mother?"

"Well, now, I can't say for sure, *Malyshka*," Uncle Misha would say, and I'd see his eyes begin to twinkle. "But, she did know your name." He'd wink then, and beneath his beard, I'd see him smile.

I'd feel all filled up with love after that, no matter how many times I heard it. Maybe one day, I'd be able to see into the spirit world somehow. Maybe I'd see the lady who had left me with the bears. Was she that beautiful spirit of calm light and pleasant smell? I really wanted to know where I had come from.

The only clue I had to her existence was a tiny necklace that was hanging around my neck. It had a locket, and inside that locket was a note with my name and birthday, and instructions to contact one Monsieur Fabrice Nolan of Geneva for my inheritance. Uncle Misha couldn't travel with a small baby in the middle of the winter, so he'd kept me wrapped in furs until spring.

"But by then, I couldn't bear to let you go," he told me. "'Next spring,' I said, 'when she's a little bigger. Then I'll take her to Geneva.'"

He said that to himself every spring for six years until he knew that he could wait no longer. He knew I needed more than bear cubs for playmates and him for my teacher. In the wilds of Siberia, we had no modern books or computers because Uncle Misha lived a secluded life and disliked technology. He said it distracted people from the real world and made them forget who they were. And though Uncle Misha could teach me many things, he couldn't teach me algebra, chemistry, and all those other subjects that kids learn in school.

So, finally he brought me to Geneva.

"Earth to Anna Sophia, earth to Anna Sophia," Lauraleigh said with a laugh. "Are you in there?" She held out a wrapped gift for me.

"Sorry... sorry! I was thinking about Uncle Misha and how he had brought me here." I couldn't believe I let myself get so lost in thought, when Lauraleigh was standing right in front of me.

Lauraleigh must have noticed how awkward I felt, because she said, "It's okay. You just disappeared for a minute." She gave me a hug, then stepped back and handed me my gift. "It's not much, and it's nothing like what your Uncle Misha always makes for you, but I thought you might like it."

I unwrapped it and tossed the paper on the floor to clean up later. I could hardly believe my eyes.

Lauraleigh had given me a book: *The Diary of a Young Girl* by Anne Frank.

Chapter 2

After I had thanked Lauraleigh about a hundred times, she said she was going back to sleep for an hour.

It was still only 5:45 a.m., and the sun was barely ready to peek over the horizon. Since there was no way I could sleep, I stepped out of my room because I wanted to go to the dormitory's highest floor and see the sunrise. Out of the corner of my eye, I saw a small package sitting on my desk. One of the Sisters must have delivered it while I was sleeping. It was from Siberia!

Ripping the brown wrapping off and not even caring that it flew to the floor, I discovered a small box. Taped to the top was a letter written in Uncle Misha's sprawled handwriting.

Mostly Uncle Misha writes his letters to me in Russian, but sometimes he writes in English. He once told me it was his way of making sure he didn't lose his ability to converse in it, but I think he does it to make sure *I* remain fluent. He spoke to me in both Russian and English as I was growing up — so, even though Russian is my birth language, I was quite comfortable with English. I think because he knows everyone speaks French at the orphanage, Uncle Misha worries I'll forget it, and then I'll only know Russian and French.

Languages are important to Uncle Misha because he believes with every additional one a person learns and speaks, they gain a new perspective of the world. He says there can never be too many visions of the world, and I'm sure he's right. Uncle Misha has always been the wisest person I've known.

I couldn't wait to read what he said in his letter.

My Dear Malyshka,

I can hardly believe the little baby I found wrapped in fur and snuggled next to bear cubs is turning thirteen years old today. Where has time gone? I do not know. I only know what a blessing you are in my life, and that I am so grateful I was guided to bring you home thirteen years ago.

I must first tell you how sorry I am that I've not yet made it to Geneva to see you in person. Circumstances have made travel difficult right now, but know you are always on my mind, Malyshka. As I stomp across the land and talk with the birds and the bugs, I wonder what my beautiful Anna Sophia is doing and thinking and learning.

Mama Bear is fine, although the mosquitos are so thick this year they are turning the sky gray and keeping her in her den. She might not even emerge to mate, which will mean no new cubs next January. But that's how brutal they are right now. Telling you this reminds me of a joke I had made up just for you. Please don't roll your eyes at your silly Uncle Misha who still likes to make you laugh even though you are nearly all grown up! Here you go:

Knock, knock.

Who's there?

Anna...

Anna-other mosquito, of course!

I had to stop reading for a minute and laugh. I could just picture Uncle Misha chuckling to himself as he wrote this, his beard bouncing up and down on his chest and his eyebrows twitching. It made my heart so happy to read his words, although it did make me miss him even more than usual.

I picked up the letter again. I was anxious to see what else he'd said.

In this box is a small gift I made just for you. It is called a dream stone. Finding a stone with a natural hole in it is rare indeed, Anna. It is said such stones offer eyes into the spirit world. I knew immediately upon finding this near Lake Baikal, it was meant for you on this most special of days.

Be well, Malyshka. Enjoy your wonderful day and remember, never fear change. If nothing ever changed, we'd have no butterflies.

All my love,

Uncle Misha.

I wondered what he meant. Did he mean now that I'm thirteen and not a child anymore, everything will change?

I decided to think about Uncle Misha's words later because I wanted to open his gift. When I did, my breath caught in my throat.

Resting on a piece of white cotton was a necklace. The chain was a thin but sturdy piece of leather I was sure Uncle Misha had made from one of the Roe deer that fed him all winter long. No part of an animal went to waste with him. Besides eating the meat and tanning the hides for clothing, he used the teeth to make buttons, the bones to make needles and knives, and the hooves to make gelatin. I'd seen him clean and process bladders and turn them into water storage containers, and transform tendons into thread for sewing. I even saw him grind up teeth and use the powder for making sandpaper. Uncle Misha always said the only way to properly give thanks to an animal who surrendered his life to you is to utilize every single part of him, and express gratitude for everything he provides.

Anyway, while the chain was soft and beautiful, it was the stone that took my breath away. I'd never seen anything like it. The way the reds and oranges and yellows swirled around each other made it look as if a brilliant and fiery sunset had been captured and turned to stone. All except for the perfectly round hole in its middle, just big enough for me to look through.

I draped the chain over my neck, and it rested so comfortably on my chest it felt like nature created it with me in mind. I wasn't exactly sure how it worked. Would I see the spirit world just by looking through it? Did I need to say magic words of some sort? I didn't know. I only knew it was more beautiful than anything I'd ever held or touched.

Wearing the necklace seemed to magnify all the electric energy I had felt pulsating through me since waking up that morning.

I remembered my idea to watch the rising sun, and I tiptoed up the stairs and slipped out the balcony door of our dormitory's highest floor. The flagstones of the balcony were cold on my bare feet, but I barely noticed.

The sky was the strange mix of pinks and purples and yellows and reds that only happen at the exact moment of dawn. I watched the colors deepen as the sun rose over the horizon as if it was welcoming me to the beginning of my thirteenth year. I felt like I was buzzing with energy inside. I leaned over the balcony, and as I did, the light of the sun reflected off the waves in my hair. It made my curls look even redder than usual. Usually, I wished for straight blond hair like Lauraleigh's, but today I was okay with just being me.

I peered at it through my new dream stone, wondering if the power of the sunrise would activate the magic in it. As the sun rose a bit higher, I squinted through the hole in the stone, lining up the light perfectly. Nothing happened, of course, but I still enjoyed doing that.

I'm Anna Sophia, I thought. *The girl who lived and played with bears, and grew up in a little cabin in the middle of nowhere with an old trapper who loves me as much as I love him.* I wouldn't change the first twelve years of my life for anything, and I couldn't wait to see what was in store for me next.

After a few minutes, the sun morphed from the colors of early dawn into a brilliant morning red. After a little more time, it turned into the soft pastel yellow of a beautiful, sunny day. I turned the dream stone to the west and found the moon, just as I knew I would: No matter how the sky changed, I could always see it. Today, it was a skinny crescent that seemed to hang in the sky from a hook. I peered at it through my dream stone — and for an instant, I thought I could see the outline of the full moon.

It wasn't until I left Siberia and met other children that I realized how odd it was to see a moon all the time. Before living in the orphanage, I assumed everybody saw the moon in its full and total state of roundness all the time, day or night.

I have always loved the moon. Maybe that's because Uncle Misha told me the spirit woman said I was born under one so full and bright it lit up all the worlds?

Because it was Saturday, classes only ran from nine until noon. Even so, they seemed unbearably long. Nobody should have to go to school on their birthday — especially one as important as the thirteenth birthday. The only thing that kept me even a little sane was knowing my party would begin as soon as classes finished for the day.

When we were finally free, I passed Gaëlle on the way back to my room. We'd shared a room at the orphanage right up until this year. That's when André and Marie Montmorency adopted her, and I moved into the Collège dorm. Now, Gaëlle was only a day student at the Collège. I missed all the nights we used to talk until we couldn't stay awake another minute. Especially, because now, we didn't seem to talk at all.

"Don't be late for the party," I called to her.

"I won't," Gaëlle said. "By the way, André and Marie are bringing a special treat."

I wasn't sure how to respond to that, but Gaëlle smiled, showing the deep dimple on her right cheek.

I had no real reason not to like her adoptive parents, but something about them didn't feel right to me. In my way of thinking, Gaëlle should have been ecstatic. After all, having parents was what we all dreamed about, and gossiped about, all the time. But while she smiled and always remained polite and friendly, something was missing. She used to have a spark in her. It used to be like part of her was on fire, and she was ready to take on the world. Now, it seemed like all those parts of her had disappeared — and I had no idea why, because she made it a point not to confide in me anymore.

I wanted to say some of this to Gaëlle but didn't. "Great," I said instead, mustering cheer that I didn't feel. "I'll see you at the beach then!"

I ran upstairs to change into my bathing suit. I could hardly wait to see what the rest of the day would bring.

Chapter 3

Downstairs, Lauraleigh and some of the other girls waited with Sister Constance.

Lauraleigh was holding a huge picnic basket, and I couldn't help but think she looked like a model in a magazine. If I could turn myself into anyone in the whole world, I'd turn myself into Lauraleigh. It wasn't just that she had long, silky blonde hair and a creamy complexion while I was stuck with curly red hair and freckles. She was also so wise all the time — and so genuinely good and kind.

I had to work on being kind, while it just came naturally to Lauraleigh. I didn't believe that even if I lived to be a hundred, I would ever be as wise or as kind as Lauraleigh was at eighteen.

"There's the birthday girl." She put down the basket and gave me an enthusiastic hug. "We've planned a great party for your special day. It's about time you got down here!"

"Now don't you be giving her airs." Sister Constance sniffed. "No need to fill her head with nonsense. A birthday is just another day like all the others."

"Yes, Sister Constance." Lauraleigh winked at me. It was like she was telling me Sister Constance could be her usual grumpy self, but we wouldn't let it spoil my special day.

We filed out of the Collège like soldiers on a march. We knew enough to walk in two straight lines. If we stumbled out of line, Sister Constance would remind us with a sharp poke from her cane.

Sometimes, I thought it possible Sister Constance didn't need her cane to walk. I had a feeling she just kept it around to poke unruly girls and remind them to behave properly. Fortunately, we all made it down the short, cobbled walkway to the beach without feeling the tip of her cane on our calves.

I immediately noticed the red convertible sports car parked near the walkway, and groaned. "André and Marie are here," I said, my tone clearly conveying my displeasure. I had hoped Gaëlle would come to the party without them.

Lauraleigh didn't like the Montmorencys either — but she, unlike me, was much too polite to ever say it. "Just be gracious," she cautioned. "No sense in making things awkward, right?"

I nodded. I could be gracious when I had to be. Most of the time, anyway.

The beach was the pride of our Collège — a private, walled-off place right on the shores of Lake Geneva. I'd spent many of my best afternoons building sandcastles out of the fine, white sand. It always amused me to know it had been specially carted in from somewhere else. Apparently, once upon a time, the beach had been rocky and covered with small, round pebbles. It just showed how much our Collège cared about small but pleasant details like that. That was one of the many reasons why I loved living there.

On a good day, such as today, you could see Mont-Blanc far in the distance on the French side of the lake. It was a glorious view, with the tall Jet d'Eau fountain sending tons of water into the blue sky far on our right. I loved this beautiful place. There wasn't anywhere I'd rather celebrate my thirteenth birthday, except maybe with Uncle Misha and Mama Bear in Siberia.

Sister Daphne was setting up a canopy with the help of some younger children. Sisters Daphne and Constance ran the whole orphanage, and they weren't just nuns; they were also real sisters. Sister Daphne once told me they had looked nearly identical when they were little. She said people always thought they were twins, which was practically impossible to believe, because now nobody would even guess they were related. Sister Daphne's cheerful face was rosy and round, and she always smelled like freshly baked cinnamon rolls and apple pie. And Sister Constance… well, she looked more like one of those old wizened dolls people carved out of shriveled apples, and while she didn't smell bad, she sure didn't smell like anything freshly baked.

"There you are, darling!" Sister Daphne cried, her arms circling me and squeezing me tight. She always gave the best hugs. "The children made you cards in class today. I'm sure you'll thank each one of them, personally."

"Of course," I said, smiling. I didn't miss her not-so-subtle hint, and she knew it.

Beatrice was jumping up and down; she was so excited to give me her card. Now almost six, Beatrice came to the orphanage when she was three. She used to follow me everywhere, and nearly drove me crazy with her constant need for attention — probably, just like I did with Lauraleigh when I first arrived. She was more independent now, and to my surprise, I found myself missing her constantly by my side. Much like I missed my late-night chats with Gaëlle.

"What a beautiful card," I said, taking it from her outstretched hand. "Why, you made me a rainbow and unicorn, didn't you?" Beatrice drew rainbows and unicorns in all her pictures.

"Yes, and that's the rainbow I'm going to follow to find my new mama and papa!" She jumped up and hugged me. "And when I find them, I'm going to tell them to adopt you too, Anna Sophia."

"Why, thank you, Beatrice. But I don't need a new mama and papa. I'm thirteen now."

I didn't know if that was entirely true, because no matter what age I was, I'd probably wish for parents. But I didn't want Beatrice to worry about finding them for me.

Two boys joined the group. The younger one, Luca, was bouncing a soccer ball and making sure everyone noticed him. The older one, Jean-Sébastien, hung back a bit. I had known Jean-Sébastien since I first arrived at the orphanage as a scared six-year-old. He had been nice to me and treated me like a little sister, making me feel less alone. We hadn't hung out much since he became a teenager two years earlier.

Sometimes Jean-Sébastien and Luca reminded me of Lauraleigh and me. Even though there was a big age difference between them, Luca being around ten and Jean-Sébastien getting ready to turn fifteen later in the summer, they were together a lot. Jean-Sébastien looked out for Luca, which was a good thing because Luca was good at getting into trouble, and Jean-Sébastien was always getting him out of it.

Luca liked to pull pranks, and although sometimes they were funny, most of the time they weren't. They were annoying. I hoped Jean-Sébastien planned to keep a watchful eye on him during my party. I wouldn't be happy if Luca decided to pull some of his not-so-funny pranks on my birthday.

"Jean-Sébastien says that thirteen is the age when girls start to become interesting." Luca grinned. Beside him, Jean-Sébastien turned ten shades of red that went all the way up to the roots of his hair.

"Is that right?" I said. "Well, that shows how little Jean-Sébastien knows, Luca. Because girls, unlike boys, are interesting starting on the day they're born." With that, I turned and left them standing there speechless, while I went to help set up lunch.

I had known Luca since he came to the orphanage when he was five, and he'd always had a little too much boy-energy for me. Jean-Sébastien could be okay most of the time. With Jean-Sébastien, it was like having an annoying big brother around.

"Luca's here, I see," Lauraleigh said, rolling her eyes a little. She passed me napkins and plates, and I set them on the picnic table.

"Thankfully, Jean-Sébastien is with him. I don't know why Luca gets invited to every birthday party when he usually ends up ruining things."

"I expect Sister Daphne doesn't want him to feel left out. Wouldn't you feel bad if you weren't allowed to go to a party everyone else was going to?"

"Not if it was Luca's party," I grumbled, but I knew Lauraleigh was right. We were orphans, but we had all grown up together, and we were our own kind of family. Excluding Luca from my party would be like excluding an exasperating little brother.

"I just hope he left the frogs at home today," I said. "Do you remember what he did at Gaëlle's party last year?"

"Oh, yes." Lauraleigh widened her eyes. "No one is *ever* going to forget that one."

Poor Gaëlle. Somehow, Luca had managed to sneak about two dozen frogs into the cooler with her cake. When Sister Daphne opened it to take out the cake, all those slimy frogs jumped out, leaping everywhere at once. Gaëlle screamed and ran as far up the beach as she could to get away from them. Later, when everything settled down, she refused to even look at her cake since it has been in the cooler with the frogs. I don't know who was more upset, Gaëlle or Sister Daphne.

I don't think Jean-Sébastien had known Luca was going to do anything like that. At least, I liked to think he didn't know. But then again, when he was younger, Jean-Sébastien used to be pretty wild, so it was hard to say for sure.

Someone cried out behind me, and I whirled around just in time to see Luca running through the sandcastle Beatrice was making. She wailed as the castle crumbled, reverting into nothing more magical than wet sand. Jean-Sébastien glanced at me and shrugged as if to say, "What can I say? it's Luca."

I glared at him and went to comfort Beatrice.

"Don't worry, Beatrice." I wiped her eyes with a napkin. "I'll help you build a new sandcastle after lunch. And one day, we'll figure out what our superpowers are, and we'll make those boys regret every mean trick they've ever played on us."

Beatrice grinned. "I want my superpower to be super-strength so I can smack Luca right in the nose!" She did a one-two punch with her fists. "I wouldn't hit Jean-Sébastien, though. He's cute."

He's only a little *cute,* I thought, surprised to feel myself blush.

What is that about? What a weird thing to think about Jean-Sébastien.

Chapter 4

"I want my superpower to be flying," I said, turning my attention away from boys and back to Beatrice.

Wishing for superpowers was a game we had played since I had first gotten to know Beatrice. I was particularly glad for it at that moment. It was a welcome distraction from the odd thought I had just had.

"I want my superpower to be super-*eating!*" Beatrice laughed. "I could eat the whole picnic, I'm so hungry."

"Well, until we do eat, I have a special mission for a superhero like you. How about you stand guard over my cake to make sure Luca doesn't sneak frogs into the cooler. You up for that?"

Beatrice let out a resounding "*yes*." Saluting me with great seriousness, she headed over to the cooler to fend off Luca, should he come within ten meters of my cake.

Lunch was a rowdy, noisy affair with everyone laughing and joking with one another. When everyone finished eating, Sister Daphne organized some games for us. She always organized the games, because Sister Constance's idea of fun was rolling skeins of yarn into balls. She was always knitting, even at the beach. She had brought along her enormous carpetbag of wool, and she spent the afternoon sitting under an umbrella, knitting a purple sweater and yelling at the boys. The strange thing was, I never saw anyone wear the sweaters she knitted. I always wondered what she did with them.

The last game we played was one in which we had to fill an enormous sponge with water from a bucket, run across the sand to squeeze it into another bucket at the far end, and pass the sponge to a teammate who would run back for more water. The team who filled their bucket first would win. That would have been my team, but Luca had stolen the sponges on the last run and squeezed the water onto the tops of two girls, Sarah and Emily, soaking them in an instant. Sarah screeched and chased him up the beach.

"You need to control your charge better!" I admonished Jean-Sébastien.

He just flashed me a crooked smile and said, "Hey, he's my friend, not my puppy. I can't keep him on a leash, you know."

I supposed that was true. Still, I wished Jean-Sébastien would start teaching Luca some manners and not just keep bailing him out of the messes he made. The older Luca got, the less cute those messes were.

By four o'clock, I was really worried about Gaëlle. *Where was she?* Their car had been sitting empty the whole day.

"It's time to cut the cake," Sister Daphne said in her usual sing-song voice.

"More food?" grouched Sister Constance from her shaded chair. "Haven't you spoiled these children enough for one day?"

"Dear Constance, that's what birthday parties are all about!" Sister Daphne laughed. "Lauraleigh, why don't you get the cake out of the cooler."

"Don't worry," Beatrice whispered to me. "I've been guarding the cooler all day, just like you asked. I'm sure Luca hasn't been anywhere near it."

I gave her a big hug and thanked her.

I tried to relax as I watched Lauraleigh carrying one of Sister Daphne's incredible creations toward the picnic table. Even though Beatrice had done her best, I was still worried about Luca ruining my cake. Where was he, anyway?

Just then, I spotted him sneaking up behind Lauraleigh with

something long and wiggly in his hands.

A garden snake! *Oh, no!*

From the expression on his face, I could tell he was going to toss it around Lauraleigh's neck. She would scream and drop my beautiful cake.

No! Without even thinking about it, I clenched my fists into a tight ball and yelled as loud as I could, "Stop!"

And that's just what everyone did: They froze. Not like in a game of Red Light, Green Light, in which people try to stand still but wobble and fall. No, I mean *everything* froze: the people, the small waves on the lake, the birds flying overhead. Even the air seemed to have stilled. Everything had frozen in mid-motion except for the garden snake. It wriggled until, with a *poof*, it changed into a billowy green scarf. As soon as it did, time started up again.

I was the one frozen now — with shock. No one else seemed to have noticed what had just happened. Luca certainly hadn't. He still thought he held a snake. He tossed it over Lauraleigh's neck, but of course, it fell harmlessly onto her shoulders. *As a scarf!*

Lauraleigh turned toward Luca and smiled.

"Why, Luca!" she said, having put the cake down. She touched the scarf draped around her shoulders. "Is this a present for the birthday girl?"

Luca's eyes bugged out so bad, he looked like a praying mantis under a magnifying glass. If I hadn't been so freaked out, I would have burst out laughing.

"Uh, no. I mean, yes," he stammered. Before Lauraleigh could say another word, he turned and ran off.

Jean-Sébastien was standing there staring at me with an odd look on his face. He appeared to know something had happened; he just didn't know what.

Had time stopped?

How could waves on a lake and birds in the sky just freeze in the middle of their movement like that? I had no idea, but I knew they did. Or I thought they did.

Except… how come nobody else noticed it?

There was no more time to think about it. Everyone was singing "Happy Birthday" to me, and Sister Daphne was pressing the handle of a knife into my hand. "You must cut your own cake, dear. It's for good luck."

Still in a daze, I cut the cake, giving the biggest piece to Beatrice and saving one for myself and one for Gaëlle, who still hadn't arrived. All the while, I kept thinking about the world around me stopping. If it wouldn't have caused a scene, I would have completely freaked out.

As we all sat on the sand enjoying Sister Daphne's cinnamon-apple goodness, Lauraleigh wrapped the new green scarf around my neck. It was soft and comfortable, and about as weird as it could be. It should have been a snake.

"Did you notice anything unusual right around the time Luca gave you the scarf?" I asked.

"Yeah, *you*. You screamed like something bit you," Lauraleigh laughed. "What was all that about? I almost dropped your cake."

"Oh... uh, sorry! I thought I saw a bee." I crossed my fingers behind my back. "But it was just a fly." I hated lying.

I would have told Lauraleigh the truth, but I was starting to wonder if maybe I had imagined the whole thing. Maybe Luca had been holding a scarf all along. Was that possible? And if so, did that mean I was going crazy?

Jean-Sébastien was still staring at me, making me nervous. "Nice scarf," he said. "Sorry I don't have a present for you." He arched one eyebrow.

"Nobody was supposed to bring presents. I just hope Luca didn't steal it from some poor woman. I'd feel awful."

"Luca can be a pain, Anna, but he isn't bad. He didn't steal the scarf." He kept looking at me. "Although I have no idea where he got it. Do *you?*"

"*Me?* How would I know?"

Before our discussion could get any more uncomfortable, suddenly and out of the blue, Gaëlle arrived. I mean *literally* out of the blue. I looked up and saw her coming toward us in a hot air balloon.

André and Marie were rich. *Mega* rich. They lived in a castle, drove fancy cars, and Marie always dressed as if she was on her way to the Swiss Music Awards. She wore more bling than the famous rapper, Jay Z. Most of the time I thought she was gross, although I would never say that to anyone except Lauraleigh.

As the giant, rainbow-striped balloon descended, I could see André and Marie in the basket, along with Gaëlle and their natural-born daughter, Candace. The Montmorencys used to say they wanted a large family with plenty of sisters for Candace. It was the reason they had adopted so many girls from the orphanage over the last several years. At least, that was what they told people.

Everyone treated the Montmorencys like they were royalty. People acted like adopting girls was the greatest charitable achievement since David Beckham donated his entire salary to children in Paris. That David Beckham thing was something Sister Constance liked to mention in front of the orphanage's patrons. I think she was hoping one of them would take the hint.

Anyway, my point was only that, apparently, I was the only person in the entire universe not enamored with André and Marie Montmorency.

Chapter 5

Last year, before adopting Gaëlle, André and Marie wanted to adopt me, but I'd refused. Everyone at the orphanage was stunned. They couldn't believe I said no because no orphan had ever turned down a family who wanted to adopt them. Especially *that* family.

"Are you crazy?" Gaëlle had asked. "I'd give anything to live in a castle and wear fancy dresses like Candace!"

"I don't need fancy dresses. And I don't need their money," I told her. "I don't even want their money."

So, instead, they adopted Gaëlle. I figured that was a good thing because Gaëlle didn't have a trust fund like I did. She needed the Montmorency's money to go to the Collège, which is private. Even though it was right next door to Luyons, it wasn't part of the orphanage, and it cost a lot of money to go to school there.

Having a trust fund had always been a mystery to me. I had never been entirely sure where it came from, although Uncle Misha once mumbled something about the spirit woman telling him she had left an extraordinarily large sum of money with Monsieur Nolan. I knew every time Uncle Misha came to Geneva to see me and ship off his furs, he also met with Monsieur Nolan. I always figured it was a courtesy thing, but sometimes — just every once in a while — I wondered what Uncle Misha did with all his trapping money.

Mostly, I thought he probably just buried it or gave it away. He had always said he had no need for it, because all money ever did was turn people into its slave. Still, there had always been this little tickle in the back of my mind that maybe he met with Monsieur

Nolan once a year because he was the one arranging for me to stay at the orphanage and attend school at the Collège.

I had thought about asking him about it, but I never have. It always felt too weird, or too awkward, or too *something*. And really, most of the time I didn't even think about having a trust fund.

Except for days when I told Gaëlle I didn't care about the Montmorency's money.

As I watched André land the fancy balloon, for about the hundredth time I thought that something felt off to me about those people. It was plain creepy how every girl changed once she got adopted into their family. And not for the better. It was like instead of parents making them happier, all the girls seemed to become sad and withdrawn. Just like with Gaëlle, they smiled less, joked less, and tried to stay away from the rest of us.

I imagined if I ever became part of someone's family, I'd want my friends to come over and share in all the joy. But that never happened — not after they became a Montmorency.

And there was an even stranger thing. After a while, all the girls seemed to move on. I could be wrong, but I didn't think anyone had ever even come back for Christmas. That was just *weird*; but none of the adults seemed concerned. Not even the Sisters Briault.

So maybe I was just being mean. Maybe once a girl became part of the Montmorency family, she wanted to forget she had ever been an orphan. Maybe, just like Sister Constance had once told me, all those girls went off to expensive universities in the United States or fancy boarding schools in France and England, and didn't come home because they were studying to become famous doctors or scientists.

And maybe my first goal as a teenager should be this: Don't be so suspicious and critical of the Montmorencys. Be more like Anne Frank.

"*Hellooo!*" André boomed.

Oh, but then there was that: André was really loud. *Ugh.*

Before I could back away, André jumped out of the basket and practically squeezed the breath out of me by locking me in a giant bear hug. All on their own, André's hugs would have been gross. But they were made way worse by the fact that he always reeked of cigars.

So much for my new goal. I tried not to visibly cringe. *Good thing I have a whole year to work on it.*

"How's the birthday girl doing?" André bellowed loud enough to echo off the Swiss Alps and bounce all the way into France.

Oh, wow. This goal might take me a lot more than a year. Out of the corner of my eye, I caught a glimpse of Lauraleigh trying not to laugh.

André started shouting something about whisking me away for a grand adventure, and I prayed Lauraleigh would come rescue me. But she didn't.

"Are you ready to go?" he said, laughing and shaking my shoulder.

"In *that?*" I asked, pointing to the balloon. I thought I was having a fine adventure on the beach, thank you very much. Floating half a kilometer above the ground in a *balloon* was not my idea of fun. I wanted to fly, but not in that thing, and not with André Montmorency.

"Of course!" Marie said, hopping over the edge of the balloon's basket without so much as ruffling her long gown.

"Candace, come out of there and let Anna Sophia and little Beatrice have a ride. They simply must see Irvigne Manor from the air."

"But, Mother, my new shoes will get ruined on the beach," Candace whined. Like Marie, she looked ready to meet the Queen of England, not attend a beach party.

"It's no problem," Gaëlle said. "They can have my spot."

"Nonsense," Marie said. "You need to show your friends how fabulous your new home is. Come, Candace. The sun is still hot enough to burn, and you don't want age spots before your time."

Candace grumbled some more, but followed her to the shade of an umbrella. "Get me something to drink," she snapped, and when nobody responded, she shrieked. "You! The little orphan in red. Get me a cold drink before I die out here!"

She had shouted to Yara, a sweet little girl just a bit older than Beatrice. I desperately wanted to tell her not to respond to Candace, but she jumped up so fast, I didn't have a chance. She grabbed a soda from the cooler, handed it to Candace, and then ran to another part of the beach as fast as she could.

Candace was rude and bossy and mean. I couldn't understand why everyone jumped to do whatever she demanded. It made me mad and I felt a strange swirling in the pit of my stomach.

Sisters Daphne and Constance Briault approached, both having missed the exchange between Candace and Yara, unfortunately. For once, I'd have loved to hear one of Sister Constance's lectures about polite behavior and good manners.

"Monsieur Montmorency!" Sister Daphne said, beaming. "How kind of you to think of the children like this. I'm sure Anna Sophia will enjoy every minute of a balloon ride. And I understand you're taking Beatrice, too. How very lovely of you!"

Beatrice was bouncing up and down on her toes, clapping her hands in excitement. "Now?" she squealed, ready to catapult herself into the balloon.

But Sister Constance placed a firm hand on her shoulder, stopping even her toe bouncing. "It is simply not proper for young ladies to ride around in such a contraption," she said, pursing her lips as she considered the balloon.

"Oh, nonsense!" Sister Daphne said. "It's marvelous."

"I promise they'll be perfectly safe," André said, not booming quite as loudly in the presence of the Sisters. He held his hand out to help me into the balloon. I couldn't think of a way to refuse without sounding ungrateful. Plus, I was not about to let Beatrice go without me and I didn't want to disappoint her. She was so excited.

"Will we be able to touch the stars?" she asked as André hoisted her into the basket.

"Don't be silly, Beatrice," Gaëlle said a little sharply. "The stars are much too high for that. And they're not even out yet, anyway." She looked away.

I was stunned by Gaëlle's tone. She had always been kind-hearted and patient with Beatrice. I'd never heard such sharpness from her toward anyone, much less toward a little girl. As I glanced her way, I noticed dark circles under Gaëlle's eyes. She looked pale and much too thin.

"Are you not feeling well?" I asked.

She gave me a small smile. "I'm just tired. I haven't been sleeping much." She leaned over and gave Beatrice a little hug. "Sorry I'm such a crab apple," she said. "Forgive me?"

Beatrice smiled, clearly relieved Gaëlle wasn't mad at her.

André climbed into the basket and lit the propane burner beneath the balloon. It made a whooshing sound like a great, fire-breathing dragon. The balloon rose as the sun began to move toward the mountains in the west. Soon, early stars would begin to peek out. I tapped Beatrice on the shoulder and pointed at the sky. "Who knows," I said. "Maybe we *will* be able to touch the stars."

Beatrice's eyes grew big. She shifted closer to me and squeezed my hand.

"You got your superpower dream, Anna," she said. "You're flying!"

I gave her a quick hug. "So I did, Beatrice. How about that."

I let the high, cool air wash over me, and I couldn't help but smile when Beatrice looked up and squealed with excitement.

After a few minutes, I got up and walked to the edge of the basket. As I leaned over it to look down, I was surprised to see how high up we were. Beatrice leaned over to look as well. She quickly sat back down and placed herself as far from the edge as she could get. I noticed her face had taken on a slightly green tinge.

"Irvigne Manor will be just over those hills," André said. "Whoever spots it first will get a prize!" He smiled, pleased with his game. André always had a pocket full of "surprises." Usually, they were hard candies so sweet they made my teeth hurt. But I supposed he meant well.

Beatrice stood up despite her discomfort. "There it is!" She pointed to a tower in the distance.

"Wouldn't you love to live in a castle like a princess?" asked André as he gave her a candy prize.

Beatrice beamed at him, her blond curls bouncing as she nodded. "I would be the best princess ever!"

As we soared closer, I saw a second tower. They were like bookends holding together the massive stone structure, which did resemble a castle more than a manor house.

"It's… big." I said. I didn't know what else to say. It certainly wasn't beautiful. It was stark and chilling, more than anything else.

"Legend says it was once the seat of the Knights Templar in this area," André said smoothly. "It's also said there are gold and jewels buried on the land somewhere, but I've not been able to find them. Not yet anyway." His grin creeped me out.

"We should have a treasure hunt," Beatrice exclaimed. She seemed to be over her earlier bout of motion sickness, but my stomach wasn't feeling well at all. I was sure that had more to do with the castle than the balloon ride. Something about it felt bad to me.

Suddenly, the dream stone grew hot against my chest. *How odd.* I got up and moved to the edge of the basket. Making sure my back was facing everyone, I grabbed the necklace and held the stone to my eye. What I saw caused my heart to begin pounding so hard I was sure my t-shirt was moving.

Darkness, a terrible darkness, surrounded the castle. It looked as if some unseen beast was blowing its black breath over and around every part of it. I could see a hot, evil blackness that was working to engulf Irvigne Manor and suffocate the life out of every living thing inside its walls.

I gasped and dropped the dream stone. I felt it clunk against my chest and realized it wasn't hot at all anymore.

It was as cold as ice.

Chapter 6

When I wasn't looking through the dream stone, I could no longer see the shadow. But that did nothing to ease the foreboding feeling I had. I looked around and was surprised nobody seemed to notice the change in my demeanor.

Did I just imagine a sinister shadow surrounding their home? I thought. *Am I truly going crazy?*

"A treasure hunt is a grand idea!" André said as he ruffled Beatrice's hair. "I bet you are full of great ideas, Beatrice. You seem like just the kind of girl to liven up that old castle." He winked at her. André and Marie made no secret of the fact that they were looking to adopt more children.

Beatrice grinned. Her big brown eyes and dimples made her adorable. Even I wanted to adopt her. I was happy she might be the next one to find a home, but a big part of me wished it would not be with André and Marie.

"Don't you think Beatrice would make a great addition to our big family, Gaëlle?" asked André.

Gaëlle nodded and gave a small smile.

There it was: that small smile. It's what made me nervous because although Gaëlle never said a bad word about her new family, I could tell she wasn't happy. I wished she would talk to me about it in private, but she always made sure we were never alone together.

"We'll be heading down now," André said. "I'm going to try and land it in the field near the gardens."

The balloon floated toward the castle, low enough that I thought we might bump into one of the towers. Beyond the house was a garden filled with statues and bushes, then a large hedge maze, and finally a big grassy field, where I hoped André would land.

"Look!" he said. "Marie has followed us to take you back to Luyons."

The red convertible was parked in the circular driveway in front of the castle. As the balloon drifted by, I could see Marie in the car along with Candace and Lauraleigh.

We were waving at them when a gust of wind came out of nowhere and tossed the balloon and basket sideways.

"Oooh!" Beatrice cried. The candy fell out of her mouth. Her eyes were huge as she watched it spiral down to the ground still far below. "Ooh, I don't feel so good."

She didn't look so good. The wind jostled us some more.

"Hang on to me," I said to Beatrice. I took her left hand, and Gaëlle took her right. André fussed with ropes and weights, trying to even us out, but an unexpected storm had come up, tossing us off course. I couldn't get the image of that black shadow out of my mind. The sudden storm felt like the shadow's arms batting us around. We were flying fast — too fast! The garden sped by in a blur; then the hedge maze and the green field that had been our original target zoomed by beneath us. Ahead loomed the edge of the forest. We couldn't land there among the trees!

"We have to land now!" I screamed.

Beatrice crouched in the basket. Gaëlle and I squeezed in beside her, trying to stay out of André's way.

"Hold on!" he yelled as he worked to turn the balloon around and head it back away from the trees. As it swerved and buckled, I felt my stomach lurch as we jerked sideways. Beatrice wailed. With horror, I saw that now, instead of heading into the trees, we were headed straight for the brick wall separating the grounds from the labyrinth. I squeezed my eyes shut and hugged Beatrice with all my might as I prepared for the crash. But we didn't crash. Instead, the basket landed with a bone-jarring thump, and my head whacked against something hard. I was sure from the way she was rubbing it, it was Gaëlle's head.

Beatrice stayed in the basket, her face all scrunched up with tears.

"Come on now," I said gently. As I helped her climb out, I told her, "You're okay. In no time at all, you'll be telling everyone what an adventure you had."

"My tummy hurts," she wailed a second before she bent over and threw up in the bushes. I held her hair away from her face and patted her back. Poor little thing!

"Well, that was bracing," André said with a small laugh of relief.

Bracing? I wanted to punch him and scream that he'd nearly killed us. In the spirit of turning thirteen, I restrained myself.

Marie and Lauraleigh were running through the grassy field towards us. The relief on Lauraleigh's face was evident when she saw we weren't hurt.

"What happened?" she asked.

"I don't know. We drifted over the house, and a sudden wind picked up." I shuddered as I pictured the black shadow.

"Just a stray wind current," André said with his usual gruff humor. His face was red, and he puffed a bit as if he had overexerted himself. "We sorted it out."

Right. You sorted it out by crashing, you maggot.

Oh, a maggot is a terrible thing to call another human being, I thought. Maybe I just wasn't cut out for setting lofty goals like thinking kindly of André Montmorency.

This was a perfect example of what I meant when I'd said being nice comes more naturally to Lauraleigh than to me.

It was a long walk all the way around the house back to the car.

Beatrice said her legs felt wobbly, so I carried her on my back. After a while, the jostling piggyback ride cheered her up, and by the time we'd reached the convertible, she looked a little more in control of herself.

"You must stay for supper," Marie said, leaning against her car.

I shook my head. So did Lauraleigh.

"Beatrice is not feeling well," I said.

"And the Sisters wouldn't like us to be away for so long," Lauraleigh added. She looked at me and winked. She had gracious down to an art.

"Well, all right," Marie said with a reluctant edge to her voice as she tapped the car roof a little too forcefully. "But we must organize a proper party so you can come see us again. Perhaps a sleepover? Wouldn't that be nice, Gaëlle?"

Gaëlle nodded, but she didn't seem enthusiastic.

"Sure," I said. I really didn't want to spend any more time at Irvigne Manor, but to find out what was bothering Gaëlle, I could put up with André and Marie for one night.

"I'm hungry," Candace announced. "Gaëlle, fix me something to eat." She waved good-bye to us and disappeared into the house.

Gaëlle rolled her eyes but followed her new sister.

"Gaëlle is such a lovely girl," said Marie with a charming smile. "She's teaching Candace how to cook. They're like two peas in a pod!"

Not even close.

I couldn't imagine why Gaëlle would put up with Candace bossing her around like that.

For the ride back, Beatrice sat between Lauraleigh and me in the backseat of Marie's convertible. She wouldn't let go of my hand. I worried that she was going to have nightmares about the accident.

"Are you sure you're okay?" I asked her.

"I'm fine now. My tummy isn't upset anymore. But I think you can have flying as your superpower, okay, Anna? I want to keep my feet on the ground." She gave me a shaky smile.

I laughed. "That's just fine. There's lots of other superpowers you can have, and still stay planted."

"Planted. That's funny," Beatrice said. "Like a flower. Maybe my superpower will be that I can turn into any flower I want." And then, for the first time in years, she stuck her thumb in her mouth. Skootching closer to me, she promptly fell asleep.

I could hardly wait to get back to my room. Between the weird snake-or-scarf thing and the balloon ride, it felt like my 4,749th day on earth was a lot more stressful and confusing than I'd anticipated. I hoped it wasn't a preview of what was to come.

Chapter 7

Dear Diary,

Two very strange things have happened already today, and I'm not even counting crashing in the balloon. I don't think I imagined everything freezing in time when I yelled the word "stop." And I know I didn't imagine the darkness I saw around the Irvigne Manor when I looked through the dream stone. Uncle Misha said it was a stone offering a window into the spirit world, so I did expect to see something when I looked through it. Just not what I saw.

My idea of the spirit world has always been that it's something beautiful. I associate it with Uncle Misha's story of finding me, and with the beautiful spirit woman whose voice sounded like it danced over glass stones. I've never associated it with something so dark and evil it made me want to throw up on the spot. But that's exactly what happened when I looked through the stone and saw the castle.

Maybe what I saw wasn't the spirit world. Is that possible? Could the stone's power also include showing me the truth about something? If so, then maybe when I looked through it, it showed me I've been right — something bad is happening there.

Unless, of course, the spirit world is like ours and contains both darkness and light, good and evil. I suppose that's possible.

I wish I had someone to ask about these things. There is just so much I don't know! Like, did I honestly stop time? If I did, then it means I also turned a snake into a scarf, and how would either of those things even be possible? They wouldn't be. But that means I've gone crazy; I've lost my mind. I think that scares me even more than the idea that, for a moment, I kept the world from breathing.

Oh. Oh, my, Diary.

What if all the things the Sisters told us about our bodies changing is true? What if I have rogue hormones or something, and they all kicked in this morning, and now they're making my brain go crazy? It's fine playing the superpowers game with Beatrice, but I've never really believed such things existed. Honestly, though, I'd much rather find out I have some sort of weird superpower than discover I'm already halfway to the Crazy Farm.

I wonder if Lauraleigh knows whether or not a girl's hormones can make her crazy. She's been a teenager for a long time; she must know. I just need to figure out how to ask her without sounding like I'm already spitting distance from the Farm's front door.

Sister Daphne rapped her knuckles twice on the door. I knew it was her because that's how she always did it: two quick knocks as a courtesy before she opened the door.

I quickly stashed my diary in the drawer.

Poking her head around the door, Sister Daphne beamed. "Hello, birthday girl!" She walked into the room. "Goodness, are you doing homework on your special day? On a Saturday, no less?"

"No way." I returned her smile. "Are you kidding?" I realized then, she had asked because I was sitting at my desk, so I added, "Actually, I was just about to write Uncle Misha and thank him for my present."

"What a lovely thing to do, Anna Sophia. Though I think it will have to wait because Monsieur Nolan is waiting for you downstairs." She gave me a wink. "I do believe he has brought you a gift."

Monsieur Nolan! He had never forgotten my birthday; not once in all the years I'd lived at the orphanage. His usual gift was a teddy bear. I think it had been his way of letting me know he appreciated how my life had begun. It was sweet, although now that I was a teenager, I hoped he wouldn't keep bringing me stuffed animals. Not that I would complain. Whatever it was, I would appreciate it. I knew how busy Monsieur Nolan was with his work as a solicitor and I was just happy he took a few minutes out of his evening to see me. If he brought me another bear, I would love it just like I loved the other six that peppered all parts of my room.

I found him sitting in the parlor of our dormitory. A cup of tea and a plate with a half-eaten piece of my birthday cake sat on the table in front of him. When Monsieur Nolan saw me skip into the room, his whole face lit up, and he pushed the plate away as he stood to give me a hug. Even though he was hired to take care of my trust fund and watch over me, he'd become as much a father figure to me as I was ever likely to have. My heart felt happy just seeing him.

"I'm thirteen!" I squealed as if he didn't know this already. "Can you believe it?"

"I can honestly tell you, Anna Sophia, that I cannot. It seems like only a year or two ago you were a tiny six-year-old who didn't speak so much as one word of French. And now look at you!" He held me at arm's length and smiled. "Flawlessly speaking French and nearly all grown up!" He gave me another quick hug and gestured toward the chair. "Please, sit. I have some things to deliver to you."

I hoped he didn't notice how dirty I was. I didn't want to tell him about the crash because he could be a little fussy sometimes. If he found out I nearly died flying around in a hot air balloon, he might have a heart attack or something, and that would be awful.

"You're thirteen today," he said, still smiling. "Such an interesting age for a young lady, don't you think?"

I smiled and shrugged, thinking "interesting" would be the understatement of the year. If I thought knowing about the balloon crash would undo him, I couldn't even imagine what would happen if he discovered I turned a snake into a scarf. If that's what I did.

Handing me a colorfully wrapped box, he said, "Happy birthday, Anna Sophia. May this be your best year yet, and one which challenges you in ways you've only dreamed of." He looked at me kindly.

"Is this from you?" I asked, and instantly realized what a stupid question it was. Who did I think he was bringing me a present from — the President of the Swiss Confederation?

"Sorry, duh. Of course, it's from you!" I laughed. Quite seriously, I said, "Thank you so much for always remembering my birthday."

Monsieur Nolan nodded, and I thought I saw a tear glisten behind his glasses.

The paper was pink and yellow and full of butterflies. It had "Happy Birthday" written in flowery letters between the butterflies. Staring at it, I thought how odd it was that both Uncle Misha and

Monsieur Nolan presented me with something that had to do with butterflies.

I tore off the paper, only this time I used great care. I wanted to save it so I would have a visual reminder not to be afraid of change.

From inside the box, I pulled out a large, fluffy, red bear. Only this wasn't like his usual teddy bear. This one had straps.

"I'm sure you're too old for toys," Monsieur Nolan said as if he'd read my mind. "So, I got you a backpack this year. It's a bear backpack for your books." His face held a quizzical expression as if suddenly he wasn't sure it was the proper gift after all.

"I love it!" I kissed his cheek. "It's perfect. Thank you so much!"

There was no way I'd ever carry my books in it; kids at school would crucify me. But I kind of liked it. It was quirky. Plus, it was a bear. I was sure I could find a good use for it.

"I do have one other package for you." Monsieur Nolan turned rather serious and formal. "I was told to give it to you after 6:43 p.m. on your thirteenth birthday."

"6:43?" I asked. "Why?"

Monsieur cleared his throat. "It is my understanding this is the exact hour of your birth."

"How do you know what time I was born?" I asked, stunned.

Monsieur Nolan cleared his throat again and made an awkward pretense of opening his briefcase. Reaching inside it, he pulled out a bulky envelope and handed it to me.

He smiled gently and ignored my question. "Since it is well past 6:43, you may open it at any time." He stood and put on his overcoat. "I suspect you will want to open it in private," he said quietly. "So, I shall leave you alone."

I sat there in shock as I watched Monsieur Nolan turn and walk toward the door. Almost as an afterthought, he came back and kissed my cheek. "Happy birthday, Anna Sophia. I suspect this shall be a most exciting and challenging year for you. Thirteen is such an interesting age."

"But—"

"I shall see you soon. Be well, my dear," he said, cutting off any questions I might ask. With that, he walked out of the parlor and toward the front door.

That was twice in an hour he had said thirteen was an interesting age. I wanted to know what he meant; it seemed such a curious thing to say. But before I could jump up to follow him, he was gone.

Chapter 8

I looked at the envelope in my hands and shook it. Nothing beeped or dinged or rang. It sounded like nothing more than a bundle of papers, although there did seem to be a rather solid object in there. Something with more weight than paper. How odd. I thought maybe Uncle Misha had sent me something else. But that didn't make sense: Why would he send it through Monsieur Nolan instead of including it in his other package?

I ran upstairs, hoping Sister Constance wouldn't see me. She never lets us run. According to her, "Proper ladies Do. Not. Run." How ridiculous! Why not? Many girls in the Collège beat the boys on track and field day. Of course, that was mostly because those boys tended to be lazy and didn't try very hard. But still, I thought girls must be allowed to run — especially when they had a mysterious package in their hands, and it was their birthday.

I made it to my room without getting yelled at, which I thought was a good sign. Once there, I sat on the bed and stared at the envelope.

I had no idea what could be inside, but suddenly my hands started to shake. The spirit lady, the one I have always believed was my mother, might have told Uncle Misha the exact time of my birth. But if that were true, I knew he would have told me before now. Uncle Misha would never have kept such significant information from me for thirteen years.

So, if this wasn't from Uncle Misha, it could only be from the one or two people who would know the exact time of my birth. It had to be from my mother or father.

Is this even possible? I thought. *Could this be from them?*

Before that very minute, if someone had told me I'd receive an envelope from my parents, I'd have predicted tearing it open fast enough to set a world record.

But I didn't.

I just sat there. I think maybe I felt shock — or maybe more than shock, what I felt was fear. I wouldn't have predicted that either, but there I was, holding the envelope that might answer questions I'd had all my life. And I couldn't open it because what if the answers weren't what I wanted to hear?

All orphans want to know about their parents. Kids at the orphanage talk about finding information about their birth parents even more than they talk about finding a new family. I was no different. For my whole life, I had wanted to know who my parents were and why I was left with a family of bears when I was only a few days old.

But what if that wasn't even true? What if Uncle Misha had invented the story about the bears to make me feel special and interesting? What if I was just a normal kid whose mother had dumped her to die somewhere, and Uncle Misha just found me? What if I'd come from terrible parents who never even wanted me to be born?

I was working myself into a real frenzy.

But then I thought I was just being stupid. If I came from awful parents, why would they send me something on my thirteenth birthday? They wouldn't!

I tore open the envelope and dumped the contents onto my bed.

I saw three items. One appeared to be a card inside a blank envelope. The other was a picture of some kind. The third item was the oddest of all: It was a spookily lifelike carving of a hand curled into a fist. I picked that object up first.

It was bigger than my fist by quite a bit. It looked like a grownup's hand, and it was so realistic it was creepy. At least it wasn't made of human skin or anything. I didn't know what the material was; it was something I had never come across before — something a little like soapstone; only it wasn't soapstone.

Very strange was the only thing I could think about the hand, so I set it on the bed and turned to the picture.

Talk about strange. Its entire left side was ragged, liked someone had ripped it out of a book; and in fact, when I glanced toward the bottom, I saw a tiny number written in the lower right corner. It *was* a page from a book! Holding it closer, I squinted to make it out, and I felt my heart skip a beat. It was page thirteen.

Seriously? *It can't possibly be a coincidence.* Things were getting weirder by the minute.

The picture looked old. Seriously old. Once upon a time, it might have been brightly colored, but not anymore. Now the colors were dull, just muted greens and browns.

It was the weirdest picture I'd ever seen.

In its center was a house on stilts, surrounded by trees. It appeared to be all by itself in the middle of a forest. A wire and post fence formed a U around the front of the house, and skulls sat on top of the posts. *Human skulls!* The instant this registered in my mind, I dropped the picture like it was on fire. As it fluttered to the floor, I thought, *what kind of sick joke is this? Really... skulls?*

I got up and grabbed the picture, feeling a little sick. I held it between my thumb and finger like it was contaminated. It disgusted me so much I didn't even know why I looked at it again, but I did. I guess I was curious.

Moving over to the lamp, I held the picture closer to the light. *Ohhh, gross!* Those weren't stilts the house was sitting on; they were *chicken legs!* Complete with gnarled feet and claws. Dropping the picture to the floor again, I shuddered and glanced toward the bed.

Do I even want to see what's inside that envelope? So far, the two things I'd examined had pretty much freaked me out.

Part of me did want to see what was in there. At the same time, part of me didn't. If this all *was* from my mother, it meant I had initially been right: She was a terrible person. Why else wouldn't she contact me for thirteen years, and then do it only by sending such disturbing things? Did I want to know this about the woman who'd given birth to me?

Of course, I might be wrong. Maybe these things weren't from my mother at all.

But, if not from her, then who?

I walked over and sat on the bed gingerly, taking a deep breath. Surely Monsieur Nolan wouldn't have brought me anything as sinister as all this felt. There had to be an explanation. I stared at the envelope for a long time. Finally, I reached out and picked it up.

This was definitely the weirdest birthday ever. I ripped open the envelope.

On the front of the card was an embossed face of a bear. I immediately recognized it as Mama Bear.

Well, okay! I thought. *What a relief — something normal and comforting.* I traced Mama Bear's face with my finger, and a profound feeling of sadness came over me. I missed her so much.

Finally, turning my eyes away from my beloved bear, I flipped the card open. As soon as I read the first line, I froze.

My sweet, darling daughter.

I couldn't read another word. I could only stare at the sudden jumble of letters written in a woman's flowery handwriting.

I'm holding a letter full of words written by my mother, I thought. *The woman who'd given birth to me on this day thirteen years ago, at precisely 6:43 in the evening, wrote me a letter.*

The feeling I had was so overpowering I nearly burst into tears… but I didn't. I didn't want to cry. Not yet, anyway. Not until I knew what she had to say.

I looked back down at the card and realized I had been holding my breath. Letting it out with a whoosh, I forced my eyes to keep reading.

My sweet, darling daughter,

If I could be with you on this most special of days, I hope you know I would be. If I could have been with you every single minute of every single day for the last twelve years of your life, know I would have been by your side. But that was not the Creator's plan for us, so I had to leave you in the care of Mama Bear until Misha could find you and take you home with him.

I looked away. *It's true!* Uncle Misha had told me the truth — my mother had guided him to Mama Bear's cave so he could find me.

I smiled and felt two silent tears slip from my eyes as I found my way back to her words.

I do not have to see you on this day to know you have grown into a beautiful girl, my precious Anna Sophia. How I wish I could hold you and look at you, my only daughter! Do you have my hair (so red and curly), and your father's eyes (so big and brown), as it appeared when you were born? I can only hope your father and I have given you the best of ourselves, and that you will never have to struggle with the lesser traits each one of us harbors.

I hope your life has been a happy one, Anna Sophia. I hope you have felt safe and loved by Mama Bear, Misha, and Fabrice Nolan. They are all entrusted to look after you. This isn't the same as having your mother — I know this. Still, I hope your first twelve years have been rich with the love of both people and animals. I hope yours has been a life that filled your heart with some of the wonders and beauty of the natural world, and of worlds beyond.

Have you felt something of the worlds you cannot see, Anna? Perhaps not yet. It is when one turns thirteen that everything begins. This is when all that began upon entry into this earthen world explodes into being. So, if you've not felt this yet, it is only because you were not yet ready. You are ready now. Of this, I am quite sure.

You were born under the light of the full moon, my wonderful daughter. Do you feel the moon's power? She watches over you always, Anna Sophia, and her power is yours to call upon. This is the gift she gave you as you slipped into this world. It is also my gift to you, for her power was once bestowed upon me.

But you also have your own powers, Anna. Those that are unique and precious only to you. As is true for all powers bestowed upon any of us, it is important to always use them wisely.

Chapter 9

I stopped reading my mother's letter.

What does she mean? I wondered. *What powers? I don't have any special powers. Is she talking about the kind of power everyone has — like the power to choose to love and do good in the world, or to be hateful and unhappy and cause people pain? But that can't be right, because she said mine were unique.*

I didn't understand what my mother was telling me. Suddenly I felt lightheaded and clammy. It felt like the air in my room had gotten too thin. It was all so much to absorb. And it was all so confusing.

I took a deep breath. And then another. I thought about how my mother had just given me more information than I'd ever dreamed I'd have. Now I knew I had her red hair and my father's brown eyes. Just knowing these two things made it worth any confusion I felt.

As I absently fingered my curls, I thought I'd never again complain about not having hair like Lauraleigh's. Knowing I had hair like my mother made me love everything about it.

But what did she mean about worlds others can't see? And what did she mean about turning thirteen and everything exploding?

Maybe there was more in the letter that would explain this. I picked up the card again and started reading.

You come from a unique and powerful family, Anna. I think over time this will bring you great comfort and joy. However, undoubtedly, it will also bring you moments of great angst and hardship. I wish I could spare you those times, but I cannot. No mother can, really. Ultimately, we alone must find out who we are, and what our place is in the world. It is only through our lessons and what we take from them, that we can find answers to the questions about our purpose on earth. Remember to embrace your quest, Anna. It is important to always embrace your quest.

Finally, know you are not the orphan you believe yourself to be, my darling daughter. Never forget that every family is like a tree where each branch is born from the same set of roots. This is what makes a tree strong and resilient. It is a tree's roots which allow it to withstand the whims of both mother nature and mankind, throughout the test of time.

So it is with each person in a family, Anna. Know you have roots. Understand they run deep and keep you bound to others, as they are bound to you. Remember this, for it will ground you and keep you strong. The day will come, my sweet Anna Sophia, when understanding this will serve you well.

There is so much more I want to tell you; so many things I wish to say! But my time is running out, and I am rapidly weakening. Only by necessity must I limit the length of this letter. Please know this.

I shall end by reminding you to continue to place your trust in both Misha and Fabrice Nolan. They alone will always place your best interests before all else. Your destiny is to do magnificent things, darling daughter, and this will be both your blessing and your curse. Because of this, it will be important not only to trust them, but to speak the thoughts in your heart to them. As my wise and wonderful friend, the beautiful poet, Sappho, says, "What cannot be said will be wept."

I have given you the items in the envelope to help you. Look at the picture by the light of the moon, and keep the hand close to you. When you need help or assistance, hold it over a flame. I call the hand Squire, and it's only fair to tell that Squire will try to tickle you and make you laugh — and laughter, my sweet Anna Sophia, is always a good thing. A joyous thing. Life will be easier and happier if you remember to live simply, speak kindly, love deeply, and of course, laugh often. I think Squire can, in time, help you with all these things.

You are my precious daughter, Anna Sophia, and I love you with all my heart.

Much love always,

Your mother, Sereda

....

Sereda. My mother's name is Sereda, and she says I have roots.

The more I read, the more questions I had. I put the card down and walked over to where the picture lay on the floor. I picked it up and stared at it, then turned and stared at the hand.

My mother said I needed both the moon and a flame to understand these two gifts, I thought. *I certainly don't have either one of those things here in my room.*

I knew that as soon as I was sure Sisters Daphne and Constance were asleep, I was going to sneak out of the orphanage. Until then, I had a lot of thoughts I needed to share with my diary. When I wrote that I might have more interesting things to tell it later, I had *no* idea how true this would turn out to be!

Dear Diary,

I can't believe I got a letter from my mother.

My mother!

I have a mother named Sereda, and I have hair just like hers. And you know what she called me? She called me her darling daughter and her precious Anna Sophia. Those were her exact words. I can hardly believe it.

It's funny, but right now, it doesn't matter quite so much that she isn't here. Now that I have this letter, it almost feels like she is here. I've already read it three times, and I know I will read it a thousand times more. I will keep it always and forever. I just hope I don't wear it out by reading it so many times.

I treasure this letter; I do. But it leaves me with so many questions it feels like my head might explode if some of them don't get answered. Like, why did Monsieur Nolan wait so long to give it to me? And why hasn't he at least told me he knew her?

I also wonder what my mother meant when she quoted her friend: "What cannot be said will be wept." What an odd phrase. Did she mean if I don't talk about the things bothering me, it will all build up and I'll end up crying? I can't imagine that happening to me — I tell Lauraleigh everything that bothers me. And when I need to, I do talk to both Uncle Misha and Monsieur Nolan.

Plus, nothing happens in my life that is so dramatic I feel a need to cry over it. I mean, yes, I'm worried about Gaëlle, and yes, we did crash in a balloon today. But usually, my life is rather boring. I get up, go to school, eat, go to sleep, and do it again. So, it's not likely that anything big would ever build up inside me.

I think I'm most curious about what my mother said about me not being the orphan I think I am. That's weird because, well, she didn't say a word about who my father is. She didn't tell me his name or anything. Just that he has brown eyes. And she didn't say if I have grandparents or anything like that. Obviously, they must all be dead because if they weren't, I wouldn't have been found with Mama Bear or have been eligible to live in the orphanage. I wonder if she meant just having a history of family keeps a person strong. Maybe she meant even if the people in a person's family aren't alive, they are all still bound to each other. It's odd. I wish she had explained this.

I suppose my mother would have told me more, and explained things better, if she could have. But it sounded like she'd written the letter right before she died, which I find to be an utterly sad and heartbreaking thought. I can't believe she used her last bit of strength, and her last few breaths, to write me this letter.

I don't even know how she died. Or why. Did she have a disease? Or an injury? I wish she could have told me these things, and so much more.

The whole thing about there being other worlds, and about me having power... it's all so strange and disconcerting. None of it makes sense. I can't help but wonder if it's all related to what happened at the beach and Irvigne Manor today.

And then, those gifts! What am I supposed to make of all those strange items she left me? A disconnected hand? Eww. And the weird picture of a hut on chicken legs? That is so gross! I don't feel like they're sinister anymore, but I'm not sure what I think they are, either.

All I can say is I hope I don't get caught sneaking out tonight. If I can find some answers to all these questions under the moon, it will be worth any risks I must take.

What an odd and curious birthday this has turned out to be. It is far better than I could have imagined, especially if I don't think about the balloon crash or the darkness surrounding Irvigne Manor.

But it's impossible not to think about the darkness I had seen. What if that's why Gaëlle has been acting so strange? What if she is in terrible trouble?

What if all the girls adopted by André and Marie are in trouble?

Is this what my mother meant when she said my destiny was to do magnificent things? Am I supposed to save those girls from evil? If I am, I have no idea how. I may have turned thirteen, but I didn't turn into a magical being with supernatural powers that will let me save the world.

I wish my mother's letter had given me that kind of power. Then I really would be able to help Gaëlle.

Chapter 10

Sneaking out of the orphanage was a little more nerve-wracking than I had expected. Sister Constance was so strict, I wouldn't have been surprised to find her sleeping in front of the front door just to make sure nobody escaped. Not that anyone ever tried to escape. We didn't — we all loved it there. Besides, where would we go?

Well, it wasn't entirely true that nobody had tried to escape. When I first arrived at the orphanage, I ran away numerous times. I would go to a beautiful park not too far away. It had the same kind of massive and ancient trees Uncle Misha had around his cabin. I was so lonesome for both Uncle Misha and Siberia, I just needed to find a place that felt like home. Once I discovered the park, I would go and sit with my back against this one very big oak tree. It was my favorite. I'd sit there for as long as I could and talk to the trees. I'd tell them all about Mama Bear and Uncle Misha.

I must have given Sister Daphne a dozen heart attacks in the first month I was there. After a while, once they figured out I always ran to the same place, Sister Daphne started driving me there twice a week. We had an arrangement: If I didn't run away on my own, she would take me and give me as much time alone with the trees as I needed. Finally, after almost a year at the orphanage, I told her she didn't need to take me anymore. The trees told me they'd be there if I ever needed them, and that was good enough for me.

Over the years, I'd returned to the park a few times, although never when it would cause Sister Daphne concern. When we'd have a free afternoon, or a few hours of free time, I'd get permission and go back to my favorite tree — the same ancient oak I first sat beneath and told of my sadness. It stands over a rock formation I named Bear Paw Boulder because, to me, it looked just like the hand of a bear.

I hadn't been to the park for quite a while, but I knew it was where I would be going with the hand and the picture.

As I tiptoed down the stairs, I avoided the second step from the top because it always squeaked. I was glad I hadn't forgotten about that. And just to be sure I was extra quiet, I carried my sneakers in my hand.

I knew Sister Daphne would be sound asleep. Unless there was an emergency, she was asleep by 9:00 every single night and up at 5:00 every morning. Not true for Sister Constance. She was always up to make sure the older girls didn't miss their curfew. Sometimes, I could hear her making rounds and checking on all the rooms. I didn't know if that was to instill the fear of her wrath in us, or because she worried about us given the recent news reports on several children gone missing around Geneva and in the neighboring areas of France. But I can tell you that when it was lights out time, everyone's lights went out.

Sister Daphne's room was downstairs and toward the back, but Sister Constance's room was right next to the parlor where Monsieur Nolan and I had been sitting earlier. It was very close to the front door, which made me nervous. I needed to be sure she was sleeping soundly before I tried to open it — because sometimes it squeaked, too.

My heart thumped in my chest as I laid my ear against Sister Constance's door. It was beating so hard and fast, in fact, I was afraid it would wake her up. Fortunately, the low and steady rumble of her snores was louder than my racing heart. I could only hope those sounds meant she was dreaming about things that had nothing to do with me sneaking out.

Hopefully, she'll keep snoring and dreaming for a long, long time, I thought as I tiptoed into the small kitchen off the parlor. We all called it the Little Kitchen, but it was more of a lounge. It didn't have an oven or stove, just a small refrigerator for keeping healthy drinks cold. It also had a hot plate with a kettle for brewing tea. Sister Constance didn't allow us to have sodas or other sugary treats, so there wasn't anything like that in there. But, that was fine — I wasn't in there to find food. I was in there to find candles and matches.

Although I couldn't remember ever having a power outage, the Sisters stored enough candles to provide light for all our rooms so we wouldn't miss any study time, just in case. Little did they know we all used the candles and the darkness to hold séances where we called upon our ancestors and tried to levitate one another off the ground. Neither of those things ever worked, but that didn't stop us from trying, or quietly shrieking when we thought we'd called up a ghost.

I was sure the Sisters kept the candles in this room. I just needed to find them without making any noise — something I was thinking might be a tall order for me. Saying I'm a little clumsy is kind of like saying a rhinoceros is a little on the big side.

Finally, in the last drawer I checked, I found the jackpot. There must have been a hundred little candles in small aluminum containers, along with several small and medium-sized candles that fit into glass holders. I had brought the bear backpack along, thinking this would be the perfect use for it. I tucked a few of each kind of candle into it. Of course, I also had the hand and picture in there as well. I was ready — and so far so good. The house remained silent.

I didn't have a key, so I left the front door unlocked, hoping luck would be on my side and Sister Constance wouldn't wake up and notice. If she did, I prayed she'd just think she slipped and forgot to lock it before going to bed. Of course, it was a ridiculous prayer because Sister Constance would *never* forget something like that.

Outside, fog had blown in from the lake — a very common occurrence for our area. It hid the town under a ghostly haze, which I thought was great. If I couldn't see anyone through the fog, no one could see me. No one was out and about at that hour, anyway — all the streets appeared deserted.

Even though it was June, the nights were still chilly. My feet nearly froze as I hurried over the damp cobblestones, and as soon as I got around the corner, I stopped to put on my sneakers. I headed toward the road leading to the park and away from the lake.

Everything seemed so much closer than when I was six. Back then, I remember thinking I had walked so far that I must surely be getting close to Uncle Misha's cabin in Siberia. But the park was only a couple of kilometers from the orphanage. Once there, it was another half a kilometer or so to get to the old forest. As soon as I saw the twisty rivulet winding through the trees, I started to run. I knew I was getting close and I couldn't wait to sit under my giant old oak and get answers to all my questions.

I just hoped the moon would come out from behind the clouds, because if she didn't, this whole risky excursion would have been for nothing.

Finally, I arrived. I took off my bear backpack and threw it to the ground. Trying to catch my breath, I sat with my back against the rough and familiar bark of my beloved tree.

I glanced around and realized my mother was right. The trees were strong, and even though each branch seemed independent of the others, it wasn't. It was the first time I had ever looked at a tree and thought about how all the branches were forever bound to one another and their roots.

I breathed in deeply and let the scent of the ancient forest fill my entire being.

My new bear backpack seemed to be grinning at me. I picked it up and opened the zipper to reveal my stash of secret items. I laid them out on the ground one by one: my mother's card, with all her beautiful words, the weird page ripped from a book with the house on chicken legs, the creepy, carved hand, and finally, the matches and candles.

The forest was on higher ground than the town, and the air was crisp and clean without a hint of wind. The fog didn't reach this high, but clouds still covered the moon.

I picked up the weird drawing and examined it again in the dim light. My mother said to look at it by the light of the moon, but it appeared the same as it had in my room. Suddenly, the clouds parted. Moonlight spilled over the page in my hand, sending my heart into instant overdrive. There was a whooshing sound in my ears — the kind that's only happened to me when I've had a massive adrenaline rush. Which is exactly what I was having because *the drawing started to move.* Not the whole page — the *ink.*

I jumped up and dropped it so fast I might well have been holding a hot piece of coal.

The page landed with the picture side up, and I stared at it in total shock. The ink glowed! I stood there and watched as it wiggled and jiggled, and then, just as if I was looking at a 3D screen, it jumped right off the page. I would have taken off running in absolute terror had I not felt strangely rooted to my spot.

The gnarled chicken legs bended and straightened, like they were having a good stretch. It made the house bob up and down.

Suddenly, the skulls on the fence whipped around so they were facing me as blue light shot straight out of their eyes. I heard an awful, hysterical cackling sound — it was a horrific laugh. I couldn't even tell from what direction it had come.

And then, my heart started beating faster than a baby bird's wings on its first flight.

An ancient-looking witch with a pointy nose and odd teeth too big for her mouth popped up from behind the house.

A strange sense of terror crept over me. There wasn't a witch in the original picture. I was sure of that. But there she was, sitting in — in something like a *bowl*. She sat in it as if it were a boat, and she held a broom in one hand. She zoomed around the house in her bowl and swept the dust off the roof tiles.

Before I could even fully process this, a ferocious wind came out of nowhere. The picture fluttered off the ground and into the air. It hovered in front of me long enough for the witch to turn away from her house and stare straight at me. Her eyes bore into mine, drenching me in a feeling of such absolute terror, I might as well have been standing in a rainstorm of horror.

As the picture blew away, I heard that awful laugh again. The sound ground into me like cayenne into an open wound, and I felt it burning all the way to my bones.

I couldn't move. Fear cemented my feet to the ground. As if by instinct alone, I willed myself to run and chased the picture as it flew across the damp grass. With no more warning than when it started, the wind stopped, and the picture fluttered to the ground. Although it was no longer moving, I pounced on it as if any second it might jump away.

When I looked, the ink was still. The witch wasn't in sight.

Whoa.

I glanced up at the moon, wondering what on earth had just happened. My pulse was pounding in my ears, and my hands were shaking so hard I could barely hang on to the picture. With a deep breath, I glanced down and felt my heart lurch in my chest.

Sitting in her bowl was the witch. This time, as she stared straight at me, her upper lip lifted and her mouth curved into a hideous version of a smile.

As if getting ready to take a giant bite out of me, her oversized teeth chomped together. Up and down. Again and again.

Chomp. Chomp. Chomp.

Chapter 11

A shiver ran down my spine, and I shuddered.

The moon disappeared behind a cloud, as if to help me. I folded the picture and tucked it inside the backpack, hoping to never look at it again.

As I moved back to my tree, questions flooded me. Why would my mother leave such a frightening present for me? What did it mean? And who was that horrible witch?

I couldn't help but wonder if both Monsieur Nolan and Uncle Misha had known my parents. If they had, why hadn't they told me? If they knew about this so-called gift from my mother, why hadn't they prepared me for it?

My eyes fell on the carved hand. My mother said if I needed help or assistance, to put it over a flame. Well, I most definitely needed both of those things. The picture, and especially that *witch*, had scared me half to death. I needed answers, and I hoped the hand could give them to me. Except, I couldn't imagine how it would. It's not like it would start talking once it got hot.

Although… maybe it would. Either way, it didn't matter. As long as it didn't turn into that witch, I didn't care. I just wanted it to tell me what was going on.

I lit the small votive candle and placed it on the ground.

I picked up the hand. It felt sort of waxy. Logic told me it should melt, but after what I saw happen with the picture, I didn't think logic meant a whole lot. I knew anything might happen.

However, knowing anything could happen, and being prepared for what did, were two very different things.

At first, putting the hand into the flame did nothing. The hand didn't melt or turn into a magic eight ball I could shake for answers to my questions. It just stayed waxy and hard and still. But then it shivered and exploded. Not like a firecracker or a bomb — it exploded in size and came *alive.*

I let loose with a terrified shriek and dropped it faster than a sword cuts through melting butter. But it didn't fall to the ground. It zipped around the trees as if it were *ever so happy* to be free.

When it completed a circle, it came back and hovered right in front of me. Out of fear, I backed up a few steps to get away from it, but it moved the same amount of space toward me. I backed up some more, and again it moved toward me. Then it stopped being a fist and opened itself up toward me. It looked just like all the hands reaching out for a handshake when two people said hello.

Are you kidding me? Is it trying to introduce itself and shake my hand? My mind really couldn't wrap itself around that thought.

It hovered there, waiting for me to shake it, but I wasn't sure I even wanted to touch it. A disembodied hand floating in the air was more than just a little bit creepy; it was *crazy.*

But it just stayed in front of me, fingers outstretched.

Who knew a disconnected hand could be so insistent on saying hi.

Not me, I thought. *For sure, not me.*

I tried to calm down by telling myself everything would be fine. After all, a mother who writes a loving letter to her daughter wouldn't send a present that would cause harm.

Would she?

Tentatively, I offered it my hand.

It grasped my hand gently but firmly, which surprised me. The sensation was strangely reassuring. It was warm and comforting, and like nothing at all I had expected. After just a few seconds, it let me go and hovered in the air once again.

I felt like I needed to say something, although talking to a floating hand felt more than a little awkward. Still, if I wanted to find out what was going on, I needed to do something other than stand there and stare.

"So, uhm… *hi.* I guess we're introducing ourselves. I'm Anna Sophia."

It bobbed in the air. I couldn't figure out if it already knew this about me, or if it was just acknowledging it.

"And you're… Squire, right?"

It bobbed again. I couldn't help but think it was going to take an awful long time to get answers if all it did was bob up and down.

"Okay, well… good." I stood there for a while, not knowing what to say, so I asked, "Are you a boy hand?"

I couldn't believe I just asked a bobbing hand if it was a boy. I felt like an idiot.

It hesitated, then floated in the air making a gesture that was somewhere between a nod, and an "I don't know."

Who knows, I thought. *Maybe disembodied hands are genderless?*

"Well… would it be okay if I think of you as a *him*? It seems a lot nicer than thinking about you as an *it*." I was feeling increasingly more stupid.

Squire nodded, and I stood there thinking how weird it was to be having a conversation with a floating hand. Although not much of a conversation, considering I mostly stood there and stared, and Squire hovered in front of me and bobbed.

Finally, it occurred to me to ask, "Can you speak?"

He turned side to side like he was shaking a "no," then he mimicked holding a pen and scribbling.

"You can *write?*" I said in astonishment. *What a relief.*

When he nodded, I smiled. "That is so great! But I don't have a pen with me."

He spread his fingers wide, which I guessed was a disembodied hand's version of a shrug.

Suddenly, I realized how tired I was. My watch said it was after two in the morning. It had been a long day; and tomorrow, I needed to study for our year-end exams, which would start the following week.

I studied the hand hovering patiently in the air. My fear had totally subsided, and I found myself enjoying the situation. He was kind of cute — in an odd sort of way.

"I have about a zillion questions for you, but no pen and no energy. I really need to go back to the dorm and sleep. Are you okay with that?"

Squire nodded.

"You'll have to stay in my backpack. It's late, but we can't risk anyone seeing you." After a pause, I added, "*Ever*."

Squire did his nodding-and-bobbing thing, except for some reason, it felt like, this time, he was laughing.

I grabbed the bear backpack and watched as Squire squeezed himself into it. He was so big that it was a tight fit. I didn't want to crumple my mother's card or the picture, so I carried those. As I made my way back to the dorm, I felt the hand squirming around in the pack. Oddly, though, as soon as we reached the edge of town, he quieted down.

"Almost home now," I whispered.

When I reached the dorm, I was relieved to find the door still unlocked. I slipped inside as quietly as I could and locked the door, but as soon as I made my way across the floor, I discovered that my shoes were damp from the wet grass. I couldn't believe I had forgotten to take them off. All I could do was hope my wet footprints would dry before Sister Constance woke up to start the day. I wasn't about to start mopping the floor at three in the morning.

Back in my room, I grabbed a notebook and pen from my desk and took off my backpack. As soon as I unzipped it, Squire popped up and zoomed around the room.

"Shhh!" I whispered sharply. "Squire! You can't get caught in here. You must be quiet!" All I needed was someone to walk into my room and see a detached hand zip-zipping around under the ceiling.

Squire stopped in mid-air and gently came back to where I was standing. He pointed to the notebook.

"Of course!" I said. "Yes, this is for you." I handed him the pen and paper.

"SORRYYY," he wrote in big, sprawling Russian letters. *"Got carried away."*

Chuckling quietly, I said, "It's okay. Sorry I had to keep you in the pack for so long."

He bobbed up and down as if to tell me it was okay.

"I want to ask you so many things about my mom, and... well, about everything," I said. "But I'm so tired, I can't keep my eyes open. Can we talk more tomorrow?" As much as I wanted answers, if I wasn't prone in the next two minutes, I was sure I would just keel over and sleep on the floor.

Squire nodded and wrote in Russian, *"Of course."*

"How do I make you small again?" I asked.

He scribbled rapidly on the paper and he held it up to me. *"Easy. Say, Squire, sleep!"*

"Well, that *is* easy," I told him. I held out my hand for the pen. He handed it to me, and then floated across the room until he was hovering over my bed. I didn't understand that at all, until I said, "Squire, sleep!" Instantly, he fell on the blankets.

Wow. Smart thinking, Squire. It would have made quite a bang on the hard floor had he fallen all the way from mid-air. Not to mention it might have hurt him.

That was, assuming a disembodied hand could feel pain. When it was asleep.

It was too complicated and way too weird. I decided I'd try to figure it all out another day.

I picked up Squire and turned him around and around. There was no sign of the animated hand who had been conversing with me for the last couple of hours. I placed him back in the pack.

Not even changing my clothes, I lay down on top of my covers and fell fast asleep.

Chapter 12

I spent all day Sunday studying. I desperately wanted to get away and wake up Squire, but I didn't have a chance. We all went to church in the morning, and in the afternoon Gaëlle and I met with two other girls from our math class for a study session. Gaëlle was stronger than me in math, which was good. With her help, I knew I'd do fine on Monday's exam.

If only I could keep my mind on math and not Squire. This was easier said than done. All I could think about was asking him a lifetime of questions I had about my parents.

Gaëlle seemed more tired than usual. I worried about her, especially since she now had a huge purple bruise above her eye.

"It's from the balloon accident," she said after our study session was over. "Don't you remember when we smacked heads? I'm surprised you don't have a goose egg, too."

I did remember smacking heads, but my bruise looked nothing like hers.

Is she lying? Her bruise looked more like someone had hit her than bonked heads with her.

"Maybe you should have the school nurse look at that?" I suggested.

"Oh, no. It's already fading." She gave me a faint smile. Along with the bruise, her eyes looked hollow, and once again I noticed how much weight she had lost.

I didn't like any of it one bit.

My grumbling stomach told me it was time for supper. We turned to walk downstairs, and I asked Gaëlle if we could have our sleepover in Irvigne Manor the following weekend.

"I feel like we haven't seen each other since the school year started," I said. "We have so much catching up to do." I wanted to tell her about my mother's odd letter, and maybe even Squire. But more than that, I wanted Gaëlle to tell me what was going on with her.

"Um, sure, I guess," she said. She didn't sound too excited, but I wasn't about to be deterred.

"Is Marie coming to pick you up?" I asked. "I'll walk down with you, and we can ask her right now."

Gaëlle nodded.

Downstairs, the dormitory parlor bustled with students coming out of their own study sessions. Sunday nights were usually quiet, except for the Sundays before final exams. Then it was as busy as a regular school night.

Sister Constance sat in her chair, knitting a royal blue sweater. She watched the flow of kid traffic while wearing her usual look of intense scrutiny. She seemed to be just waiting to catch the student who so much as *thought* about breaking a rule. I'm sure she was disappointed no one was doing anything wrong.

Marie had parked her red car right outside the dorm, blocking the way. Apparently, she didn't care because she stepped away from it as soon as she saw us.

"*There* you are, darling!" She swooped over to Gaëlle and smothered her with a hug I was pretty sure Gaëlle didn't want.

Marie was wearing a flowing skirt in jewel tones of red, green, and blue. She had a gauzy black shawl thrown around her shoulders. That shawl gave me the creeps, although I couldn't say why.

"Um, Anna Sophia and I were wondering if we could have a sleepover on Friday night," Gaëlle said, untangling herself from Marie's grasp.

"What a perfectly *splendid* idea!" Marie exclaimed, her voice containing more enthusiasm than seemed necessary. I noticed she had plucked her eyebrows into two thin, arching lines. They looked so weird it was hard not to stare at them.

"Why don't we plan an end-of-the-year party for *all* your friends?" She wrapped the shawl around Gaëlle's shoulders. Its blackness encased her like a dark shadow. I shuddered, horrified to think it resembled the evil surrounding Irvigne Manor.

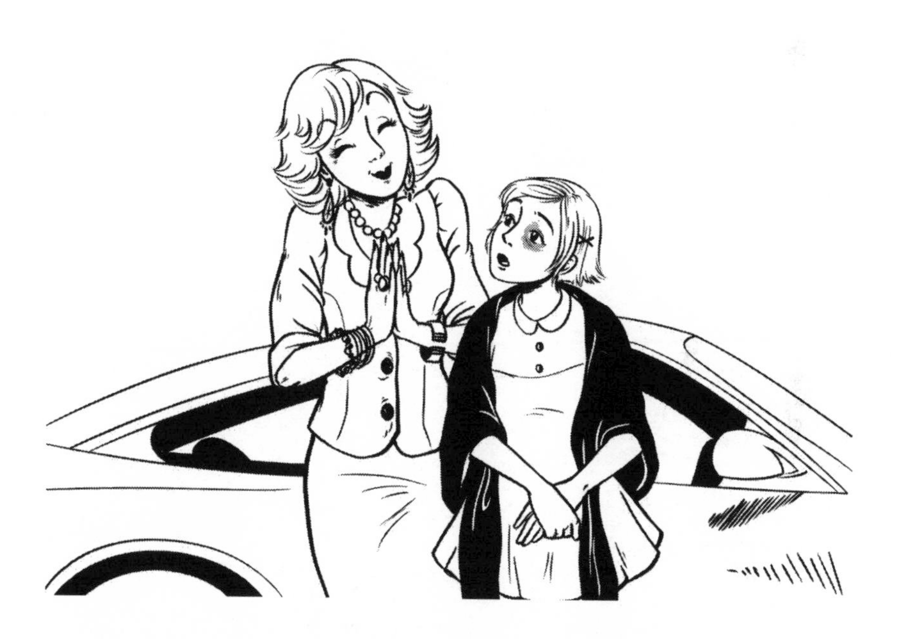

Gaëlle frowned. The giant black shawl dwarfed her and made her appear even smaller and frailer than she already looked.

"I was hoping it could be just us," I said, trying to rescue Gaëlle, who seemed too timid around Marie to speak up on her own. "We really just want to be alone so we can catch up on each other's lives."

I think Marie furrowed her eyebrows, but it was hard to tell now that they were so thin.

"Of course," she said. "You big girls don't always want the little ones around. I understand. You probably want to talk about boys, don't you? Ha! I remember exactly what it was like to be your age."

Oh, gag.

I nodded, although it wasn't at all what I wanted to talk about with Gaëlle. I wanted to talk to her about why she looked like a ghost who was wasting away.

As hungry as I was, I raced through dinner because I needed to sneak into the cafeteria and swipe a candle and some matches. I figured it would be easier than sneaking them out of the Little Kitchen again. Especially because Sister Constance was still awake.

Sister Esther, the school's cook, seemed exhausted after serving up hundreds of meals for the students. She was short and plump, with a wrinkled face that always made me think of one of those cute, little Shar-Pei dogs. She was as sweet as one of those little dogs, too. I hoped she didn't catch me; I would feel bad if she thought I was sneaking around and looking for something in her kitchen.

Fortunately, she was dozing in a chair by the oven, with her puffy chef's hat pulled down over her eyes.

I tiptoed past her and opened several drawers before finding a book of matches and a candle. I stuck both in my back pocket and headed for my room.

I said goodnight to all my dorm mates, yawning dramatically so they would think I was super tired and going right to sleep. In truth, if I hadn't wanted to talk to Squire, I probably *would* have gone right to sleep.

Once back in my room, I locked the door — something we almost never did on our floor.

With a pad and pen next to me, I lit a match and held it to a candle. I placed the lit candle on the table and reached for Squire.

A knock on my door startled me.

I opened the door just a crack and saw Lauraleigh standing there. She was frowning.

"I smelled burning matches or something," she said, trying to look over my head into the room.

Lauraleigh was our hall monitor and it was her job to keep us younger girls in line. She was supposed to report any misbehavior to Sister Constance. Although she was generally lenient, fire was never allowed in the dorm rooms. Well, except for during those theoretical winter blackouts that never happened. Since it wasn't winter, and we weren't having a blackout, I knew Lauraleigh would be upset if she saw a burning candle in my room.

"You're not smoking, are you?" Lauraleigh asked, and sniffed the air in front of my face.

"Of course not. Are you kidding?" I tried not to show how nervous I was by laughing a little bit. "You know I'd never do that." I must have really sounded nervous because Lauraleigh pushed my door open and walked into my room.

"What's that?" She pointed at the candle.

"It's a votive."

"I know it's a votive, Anna Sophia. I mean, what are you doing with it? You know we can't have anything like this in our rooms."

I wracked my brain for an explanation. "I know. It's just that every year around my birthday, I light a candle for my mother. I never knew her, but this feels like a good way to honor her."

I don't usually lie, but I had to admit, that was pretty quick thinking on my part. Normally, I told Lauraleigh everything. It just felt like until I knew more about Squire, I shouldn't tell anyone about him. Not even Lauraleigh.

Her face softened. She was an orphan too. She understood the need to make a connection to parents we never knew. To have rituals.

"I never knew you did this," she said gently.

I shrugged, trying my best to look sheepish instead of guilty.

"Well, just make sure you blow it out before you go to bed." Lauraleigh gave me a quick hug. As she started to open the door to leave, she turned and said, "It's a nice gesture, lighting a candle for your mother."

Now I felt totally guilty. Lauraleigh thought I was doing a nice thing when what I was really doing was deceiving her.

Maybe I should wait before animating Squire again. It was bad enough to have just lied, but I suddenly had a vision of him zooming around the building, trying to make people shake hands. Sister Constance would probably try to beat him with her cane, while Sister Daphne would likely have a heart attack.

I so badly wanted to know more about my mother, but it wasn't the right time. I could feel it. I blew out the candle and put Squire away for the night.

I'll go back to my special place in the forest and do this right, I thought. *No sense in waking him up now.*

At least, not until I know him better.

I had just about finished studying for my grammar exam, when Jean-Sébastien showed up. I shouldn't have risked sitting in the open courtyard between the Collège and the orphanage, but the sun was shining, and I just didn't want to be inside anymore. It was just as effective to conjugate verbs in the sunshine as it was in a stuffy, old room. The only problem was, I had brought Squire with me and was using him as a paperweight.

"Cool paperweight," he said, grabbing Squire off my open grammar book.

"*Hey!*" I swiped at his hand, but he held Squire out of my reach. "Jean-Sébastien; come *on!*" I said. "Give it back."

He laughed and examined the hand before handing it to me. "No need to freak out, Anna. I wouldn't steal your childhood playmate away from you."

I rolled my eyes. "He's hardly my childhood playmate."

I sort of had the urge to tell him it was a birthday present from my mother, but I didn't. It felt too personal. I didn't want Jean-Sébastien making fun of the fact that the only time I'd ever heard from her, she gifted me a carving of a knuckled hand.

"Shouldn't you be studying?" I asked. "You have exams this week, too."

"Yeah, I do. I'm good. It's all up here." He tapped the side of his head.

"Well, if you'll excuse me," I said, "I still need to study." I didn't want Jean-Sébastien hanging around and asking me a lot of questions. I held my book in front of my face, hoping he would take the hint and leave. When I lowered it a few minutes later, he was gone.

Chapter 13

Grammar had always been my favorite subject. Usually, I couldn't get enough of punctuation or verb conjugations, but after the interruption with Jean-Sébastien, I couldn't concentrate. It wasn't verbs I wanted to know about. It was my parents.

I looked up and saw the moon glimmering like a perfectly round opal in the afternoon sky. It's so sad all my friends could only see her at night. I felt so lucky to be able to see all of her, all the time.

I looked up and whispered the only famous line I'd ever memorized. It was from a poem by Edward Estlin Cummings. Sister Mary Catherine had read it aloud in our English Literature class early in the school year. I loved it so much that, after class, I asked if I could copy it down. I kept it in my desk the whole year.

I'll probably keep it my whole life, I thought. *Right along with the letter from my mother.*

I whispered, almost like a prayer:

> *"Yours is the light by which my spirit's born,*
>
> *You are my sun, my moon, and all my stars."*

As if in response, the moon glowed a little brighter. Out of the corner of my eye, I saw a glint of her light bounce off Squire's knuckles.

It was the only sign I needed.

I put my books and Squire in my pack, and left the gardens. When I reached the gate, I hesitated. Leaving the Collège grounds during school hours was not allowed. In our school handbook, it's listed as an offense meriting a suspension. Which, of course, would have been true for the other night, as well. Had I been caught.

I couldn't imagine explaining a suspension to Monsieur Nolan or Uncle Misha. The very thought mortified me, but I didn't stop. I hadn't gotten caught the other night, and I wouldn't let myself get caught now. It was just that simple. What I had to do was more important than anything. It was more important than conjugating verbs. It was even more important than following the rules. And not because I didn't think rules were important — I did. But for this *one* time, breaking a rule would be worth any price I had to pay. It would be worth it because Squire was going to answer questions about my parents.

I glanced around in every direction twice. Then I opened the gate and dashed down the path.

I made it through town without being spotted only through a stroke of luck. Or maybe it was due to moon magic. A week ago, this thought wouldn't have crossed my mind. But a week ago I didn't have a disembodied hand in my backpack who could talk to me using a pen. A little moon magic keeping me invisible seemed more than likely.

As soon as I passed the shops, I sprinted all the way to the road. Then I ran down the road to the path leading into the park. And I kept running — all the way through the park and to the bridge, across the bridge and to my big tree. At that point, I collapsed in a heap next to Bear Paw Boulder and tried to catch my breath.

Clearly, I was meant to be a marathoner, not a sprinter. I gulped air in big, heaving breaths, wondering if I would ever breathe normally again.

I was on my knees, with my hands on the ground for support, and sucking oxygen for all it was worth when I spotted the candle.

It was still tucked under the bushes, right where I had stashed it to make room for Squire in my pack.

I took it as a sign that if I could ever breathe again, I'd finally get answers to all my questions.

Finally, I stopped heaving. Once I realized I wasn't at imminent risk of passing out, I stood up and looked around. I didn't see or hear anyone, which surprised me considering it was a beautiful June afternoon. I took it as another sign I was doing the right thing.

I went over and retrieved the candle. It was fortunate I had thought to stick the matches inside the glass. I would not have been happy if I had taken such a huge risk in getting there, only to discover I had no way to wake up Squire because of wet matches.

After glancing around one more time to be sure nobody was near, I lit the candle and pulled Squire out of my pack. Holding him over the flame, I watched closely. I wanted to see the exact second when he turned into a live hand. But, just like the last time, there was a loud *pop* and I blinked, missing the moment. One second he was an inert carving, and the next he was bobbing and floating in front of me.

Except, this time, he dove right at me.

Poke!

One of his fingers poked me in the side. Then he zoomed back and waited, bobbing like a buoy on high seas.

"What was that for?" I asked.

He dove again, poking me in the ribs. Then again.

"Stop that!" I laughed. "It tickles!"

Squire bobbed up and down as if he was laughing too. And that was when I remembered the warning in my mother's letter: Squire likes to tickle!

Maybe it means he likes me, I thought, giggling as he poked my ribcage again. But then, I had a thought that made me stop laughing.

Squire used to tickle my mother. He used to do this very thing to my mom.

Funny, I'd never used that word before. *Mom*. Whenever Lauraleigh and I, or even Uncle Misha and I referred to her, it was as my mother — as in, "Do you ever wonder about your mother?" Or, "Was my mother the spirit that guided you to me?" But thinking about Squire tickling her made her seem less abstract and more real. More playful; more like a mom than a mother.

A warm, happy feeling rushed through me. *I have a mom.*

"Did you play like this with my mom?" I asked Squire. He was floating patiently in front of me, almost like he knew why I had stopped laughing.

He swooped in a little closer and bobbed up and down, nodding.

"I brought a pen and some paper this time," I told him. "Will you answer some questions?"

Squire nodded and hovered in the air.

I pulled out my three-ring binder and flipped to the last section where I kept blank paper. I laid the pen across the page and watched as he swooped down and grabbed it. It was so odd to see a hand floating in the air and holding a pen as it got ready to write. I wondered if I'd ever not be shocked by the sight of it.

There was so much I wanted to ask, it was hard to know where to begin.

"Let's start with easy stuff," I said. "What was my mother's name?" It's not that I was testing him. It was more like I wanted to be sure we were talking about the same person.

Squire wrote quickly. His handwriting was beautiful. It looked like calligraphy with all the letters fat and rounded and with lots of swirling tails.

"*Malyshka,*" he wrote in Russian.

"Malyshka?" That's not right. That's what Uncle Misha calls me. That's not a name, Squire. It's more like a Russian endearment — like calling someone 'sweetheart' or 'darling' or something."

Squire nodded.

"Well, was that someone's pet name for her?" I was thinking this might not be as easy as I thought it would be.

Squire bobbed, nodding.

"Do you know her real name? You know, her given name?"

It was like watching a ballet of letters swirl across the page as Squire penned, "*Sereda.*"

I felt my heart skip a beat. He did know my mother!

"And my father? Did you know him too? Can you tell me my father's name?"

Squire shook from side to side so fast I felt a slight breeze.

Whoa.

"Do you not want to tell me my father's name, Squire?" I watched him rock in a frenzied sort of way, clearly conveying how uncomfortable he felt.

Or is it fear he feels? It was all so odd.

I feared that if I asked him why he was so upset, he'd stop answering questions altogether. So, even though I wanted to know more, I decided to change the subject. I figured I could come back to the topic of my father another time — sometime when Squire was less… skittish.

Or when he knew me better and trusted me to hear whatever it was he didn't want to tell me now.

Chapter 14

I stared at Squire, wondering what I could ask that wouldn't agitate him further. I figured it would be best to act casual and pretend his hand-tantrum was no big deal.

"It's okay, Squire," I said, "We don't have to talk about my dad."

He stopped rocking but stayed high above me in the air.

"How about if you tell me where I'm from." I figured that would be a safe and easy territory.

He swooped down and glided over to the notebook. In his elegant letters, he wrote: "*Russia.*"

"Right," I said. "You're right; I am. And where are you from?"

"*Home.*"

"Home?" That was a curious response. "Where's home?"

"*With Knight.*"

Knight? I felt like I was playing a word game without knowing the rules. Nothing made sense and I wondered if Squire was just messing with me. Maybe he didn't really know anything about my mother other than her name, or maybe he was just trying to confuse and distract me for some reason.

"Who is Knight?" I asked, hoping to either trap him in his game or get to the bottom of things.

"*My other half. The left hand to my right.*"

"The le— oh, wow, of course. I get it!" Squire wasn't trying to confuse me at all. He was one of a pair of hands, and the other was missing. That made sense. Well, it made sense given the context. "Is Knight still at… home?"

"*I don't know,*" he wrote.

"You mean you don't know if he's home, or you don't know where he is?"

"I don't know where he is." Squire paused. *"I miss him so much."*

He hung limply in the air. Gone was all the animation he usually displayed, and instead, he appeared depleted of energy. Even though he was a hand, I could sense how genuinely sad he felt. I even understood it. When Uncle Misha left me in Geneva and returned to Siberia, I felt like part of me was physically missing. It must be even worse for Squire because hands are, well, they're a pair.

It crossed my mind that if I ever tried to tell Lauraleigh about this, I'd sound deranged. There was no way I could tell her about carrying on a conversation with a disembodied hand who was sad because his other hand was missing. Well, at least not without sounding like I'd turned thirteen and blown a gasket in my head.

Casually running my fingers through the grass, I said, "Sister Daphne always says it's good to be a team. 'Together Everyone Accomplishes More,' is what she says. You know, T-E-A-M, *team*."

Squire drew a big question mark on the page.

Apparently, Sister Daphne's phrase didn't make sense to a hand.

"Well, what I meant was... maybe we could work together as a team and accomplish more together than alone. I could help you look for Knight, and you could tell me things about my mother. Would that work?"

Squire nodded his fist up and down in an enthusiastic yes.

"Great!" I smiled, hoping to keep our good momentum going. "Let's start with where my mother lived. Can you tell me that?"

Squire fluttered in the air silently.

"No? Well, how about how old she was. Do you know how old my mother was when she died?"

Nothing.

"She *did* die, right?" I heard how frustrated I sounded, but I couldn't help it. It didn't help that Squire nodded lightly, but, again, wrote nothing.

"Squire!" I said more sharply than I'd intended. "My mother gave you to me to help me, but you are not helping me at all!"

He swooped back to the notebook. "*I'm sorry. Ask me something different.*"

I rolled my eyes. This was not going well. "Okay. How about this: Why did my mother write that now that I'm thirteen, things will explode into being. Do you have any idea why she said that?"

I watched as Squire scribbled words across the page. When he was done, he held it up for me to see.

"*Because, Anna Sophia, you are a witch. And witches come into their magic on their thirteenth birthday.*"

I stopped breathing, quite literally. The whole world started to spin around me, and at the same time it felt like the earth dropped from beneath my feet. I slid to the ground, inadvertently grasping the dream stone as it dangled from my neck. It felt warm.

"Th—that's not true," I meant to cry it out — only, for some reason, it came out as a whisper. "That can't be true."

My voice sounded strange. Choked. Like all the words had gotten stuck in the back of my throat. I tried to breathe, but couldn't. The edges of each breath were jagged and irregular, and if I inhaled too deeply, I was sure each exhale would feel like razors slashing through the tendons in my throat.

I think, deep down, I knew it was true even though I didn't want it to be. I wanted things to be normal. *I* wanted to be normal — a normal teenager, just like Lauraleigh and everybody else. But after those four words, "you are a witch," I knew nothing would ever be normal again.

Squire flitted from side to side in front of me. I think he was afraid I might faint.

"It can't be true, Squire. Witches aren't even real."

Maybe if I said that enough times, I would believe it.

He shot back to the notebook and scribbled something across the page. When he finished, he ripped it out and brought it over to me. *"Witches are real. You're a witch. Your mother was a witch. And your grandmother is—"*

Before I could finish reading, a violent gust of wind blew through the trees and snatched the paper right out of my hands. Another cold and angry surge of air slammed the notebook so hard against the ground, the three rings popped open. A third one ripped all my study notes out of the binder and blew them in every direction.

"My papers, *no!*" I screamed as I jumped up. I twisted and turned my head in every direction as the pages scattered across the ground and whipped between the trees.

All my hard work, I thought, panicking. I needed those pages to study for my exams. Instinctively, without thinking, I yelled, "Freeze!"

And they did. Everything did. The papers — some in midair, others standing on end in the grass — instantly became still. I couldn't feel so much as a baby's breath of wind because, apparently, the wind had stopped as well.

"What the—?" My heart was pounding against my chest.

This is exactly what happened at the beach, I thought, *when Luca was about to ruin the party.* But how was this possible? I looked at Squire, who was bobbing gently.

"You're not frozen," I said. "Why?"

He gestured at the papers in their various positions. Then he started to pick them up and put them inside the notebook.

I squeezed my eyes shut and opened them again. I hoped everything would be back to normal — but of course it wasn't, because I hadn't imagined it. Papers were still frozen, just like they had been a second before. And Squire still raced around, grabbing them in his one hand.

"Thanks, I… I, um, Squire, I…"

I knew I sounded incoherent. And I knew I was acting like an idiot. But I couldn't help it. I was in shock, and all my thoughts bounced around inside my head like popcorn in a kettle.

I mentally slapped myself. I needed to pull it together and at least help Squire collect my papers.

Taking a deep breath, I glanced around. It was all so bizarre — papers hung motionless here and there, as if plastered against the world's cleanest window. I plucked two out of the still air before grabbing three more from the grass. The way they stood on end made me think they had been frozen in a pirouette.

Soon, we had all of them — at least, all that I could see. I told Squire I'd put them back in order when I got to my room. For now, I just wanted to ask him some more questions. I stacked all the blank pages in a pile and handed him the pen, which I found resting against Bear Paw Boulder.

I felt a hint of wind and realized that, once again, the world was breathing.

"What's going on?" I asked him. "Why is all this happening?"

I watched his words dance across the page. The same words he had written earlier.

"You are a witch, Anna."

I dropped my head into my hands and groaned. "Squire—" I let his name dangle, unsure of what I even wanted to say. A million memories hurdled through my mind in a single instant: Riding on Mama Bear's back through hundreds of kilometers of tundra. Being able to see the full moon any time of the day or night. Having bear cubs as my playmates. Stopping time at the party. Changing the snake into a scarf. Seeing Irvigne Manor through the dream stone.

Having a conversation with a hand.

I heard a deep groan come from somewhere in my chest and I felt Squire's hand gently patting me on the shoulder. *He's trying to comfort me.* And even though I'd just had the shock of a lifetime, the gesture was so sweet it almost made me cry. I looked up and faced him.

"It's true, isn't it? I'm a… a… witch."

Squire nodded.

I sat there quietly, saying nothing for the longest time. A thought blasted through my mind, causing me to jerk my head upward. "Squire!" I said. "On that paper… the one that blew out of my hand—"

He was so still in the air in front of me. I was afraid I had accidently caused him to freeze in place, but he gestured for me to continue.

"You wrote that my mother was a witch, and something about my grandmother, but I didn't get to finish reading the part about my grandmother. Squire, did you say my mother *was* a witch, and my grandmother *is* a witch?"

Squire nodded.

"*Is* a witch, Squire? As in, *still is?*"

He nodded.

Oh. Wow. *I have a grandmother.*

Who is alive.

That's why my mother wrote I'm not the orphan I think I am. It's because I'm not totally an orphan. I have a living relative. I have a grandmother.

Who is a witch.

Just like me.

Chapter 15

*ear Diary,*

I'm so sorry I haven't written to you all week. I didn't do very well in my effort to be like Anne Frank, did I?

It's not because I didn't have a lot I wanted to write you; I did. It's just this was exam week, and we all studied together so late every night. By the time I'd get back to the room, I'd be asleep in five seconds flat.

Unfortunately, right now I hardly have any time to tell you anything, because Marie will be here soon. I'm finally having my sleepover with Gaëlle tonight, and I'm so glad. Hopefully, I'll be able to find out what's wrong with her. Although, who knows. She barely talked to me this whole week. And when she did, it was only to say something about what we were studying. It was so strange, and so unlike the old Gaëlle.

Still, I'm optimistic she'll talk to me tonight. It will be our first time alone together in… well, in what feels like forever.

On another important subject: I'm still trying to process what Squire had told me about being a witch. Part of me dismisses it as ridiculous. I tell myself there are no such things as witches. Then I remind myself who gave me this information — right? So, unless I'm willing to say Squire isn't real, I'll have to accept that witches are real.

And that I'm one of them.

Oh, wow. This is truly hard to wrap my mind around.

How am I even supposed to know how to be a witch? It's not like I've ever been around one! This sure would have been a lot easier if my mother had stuck a how-to manual in her letter.

Well, I'll say this, Diary. If I do have powers, I hope I use them to make the world a better place. Anne Frank was so brave, and yet, the world she lived in was awful. She died in a concentration camp, and she was only fifteen. It's so horrible and sad to think about that. One thing is for sure: Through her diary, she has provided so much inspiration to people — me on the top of that list! I'll work hard to be more like her, and if I have special powers, I'll do everything I can to make the world a better place, so nobody ever goes through what she did again.

There's another girl I found out about, who is kind of like Anne Frank. Only different. Her name is Malala Yousafzai. She's Pakistani, and she was shot in the head when she was only twelve. They tried to kill her because she spoke out about the importance of girls attending school. Malala was even younger than me when this happened — but, like Anne Frank, she's so much braver than I could even imagine being.

Malala wrote a book, too, but it isn't a diary. It's a memoir about what happened when she was shot, and after. I especially remember something Sister Mary Agnes read from it. It's what Malala said about fear. She said: "I am stronger than fear."

I'm afraid of being a witch, but if Malala Yousafzai can say she is stronger than fear after being wounded in the head, I should be able to feel that way about my own life which is blessed and full of privileges she'd never had.

Well, maybe not yet, but I can work toward feeling that way, right?

I wonder if all this is what Uncle Misha had meant when he'd said not to be afraid of change. Is this the quest my mother had told me to embrace? Am I going through the same type of experience as a caterpillar when it transforms into a butterfly?

I wish I knew.

•❦•

I put my pen down with a sigh and blew out the candle that I had dared to use to write my Diary entry.

I was so tired from all the exams, and even from all the worrying I had been doing all week. It didn't help that Jean-Sébastien spotted me when I came back from the forest on Monday. All week I worried he would rat me out. He didn't, but every time he saw me he gave me a look that I interpreted as, "Be careful, Anna Sophia… I could turn you in anytime I want."

He was so infuriating.

I looked around the room. It was getting late, and I had to get ready for the sleepover. I decided to put everything I needed in the bear backpack because I thought Gaëlle would get a kick out of it. As I filled it with my pajamas and spare clothes for the next day, I thought about taking my mother's letter — but then I decided I'd just tell her about it. I didn't want the letter to leave my room unless it could be with me the whole time.

I threw my toothbrush in the pack, and at the last second, I put Squire, a candle, and some matches in there as well. If I did tell Gaëlle about the letter and finding out I'm a witch, I might need Squire to prove I wasn't lying or going completely crazy.

As soon as I got downstairs, I saw Lauraleigh. Sister Constance was giving her a lecture of some sort. Moving closer to find out why Lauraleigh, of all people, was being subjected to one of Sister Constance's sermons, I heard her say, "You drive the speed limit, young lady. Not a kilometer faster." Sister Constance pounded the floor with her cane for emphasis. "And you have these girls home by ten tonight, or this will be the last time I agree to such nonsense."

Lauraleigh was getting to drive her car somewhere? Lauraleigh didn't have a trust fund like I did, but she did have a grandfather who very much wanted her to join the family business when she graduated high school, which was at the end of this month. It was the business her dad would have taken over had both he and Lauraleigh's mother not been killed in an accident when she was five. When Lauraleigh got her driver's license last year, he'd bought her this car to cement her allegiance to him.

It was mean for me to think this way, but it wasn't like he came around all that much or paid a whole lot of attention to her. I couldn't help but think the car was his way of making sure when he got too old to run it, the business would stay in the family. I supposed it wasn't my place to criticize him for that. But still, I always thought of the car as his way of bribing Lauraleigh, when all he had to do was ask her, and she would have agreed to take over the family business. Even if she didn't want to, she would have agreed to it. That's just the way she is.

Of course, it hardly even matters that she had the car. Sister Constance almost never let her drive it anywhere.

I wondered where she was planning to go that she would be taking girls from the orphanage with her. It must be somewhere special; they were all dressed in their Sunday best.

As soon as Sister Constance finished her speech and walked away, I went over to Lauraleigh. "You look so pretty," I said. And she did. She was wearing a deep blue dress that complemented her long, pale hair. I was just about to wish I had hair like hers, when I remembered I wasn't going to do that anymore — not now that I knew I had my mother's hair. I guessed it was going to take me more than six days to remember that.

"Where are you going?" I asked. "You're so dressed up!" Three girls from my floor stood nearby, fidgeting. It was obvious they wanted Lauraleigh to hurry up so they could leave.

Lauraleigh glanced at me curiously. "To André and Marie's. Were you not invited?" She sounded surprised.

"Uh, yes, I was. But I thought—"

I thought I was going to have a quiet night alone with Gaëlle like we had planned. I should have known better. Whatever Marie wanted, Marie got. And clearly, Marie didn't want Gaëlle and me to have too much time alone together. The question was, *why?*

The feeling of something amiss at Irvigne Manor returned in full force.

"You're all going there?" I asked, although I already knew they were. Why else would they all be dressed in their fanciest clothes?

"*Everyone* is going!" a girl named Jodi chimed in. She rounded her eyes. "Aren't you going to change into your good clothes? It *is* a castle, after all!"

I was about to say no; I wasn't going to change my clothes. I was about to say the plan had been to spend a night *alone* with Gaëlle, and I had no need to dress up for that. But before I could say a word, Marie stuck her head inside the front door.

"*Yoo-hoo!* There you are! We've been waiting for you out here, Anna."

I felt a sense of dread. It felt as if the dark shadow I'd seen through the dream stone had begun to spread its tentacles around me again. I shivered.

Lauraleigh noticed my discomfort. Placing a gentle hand on my shoulder, she whispered, "Are you okay?" Her eyebrows raised with concern.

"I'm fine." I pretended to smile. Turning to face Marie, I said, "I'm on my way."

"We'll be right behind you," Lauraleigh said as she watched Marie walk out the door. I could tell my fake smile didn't fool her at all.

"I'm glad you're going," I said, and I meant it. Even though I had wanted time alone with Gaëlle, the fact that Marie had organized a big party felt creepy to me somehow. It made me feel less apprehensive knowing Lauraleigh would be there.

When I got outside, Beatrice was in the front seat of the red convertible and Sister Daphne was standing beside the car.

"There's our girl!" Marie beamed, acting like she hadn't just seen me two seconds earlier. "But you forgot your party dress! No matter. I'm sure I have something just your size at home. We'll have fun dressing you up, won't we?"

"We sure will." I opened the rear door and got in the car.

I was positive my sarcasm went unnoticed, since Marie didn't ever seem to pay attention to anyone other than herself. Fortunately, Sister Daphne was busy with Beatrice because she sure would have called me out for being sarcastic.

"You'll keep an eye on Beatrice, won't you, dear?" Sister Daphne asked. "Make sure she doesn't eat too many sweets."

"Of course. I'd be happy to," I said. I was extra polite in case she actually *had* heard me and was just being nice by not admonishing me in public.

I sat in the car, while Sister Daphne gave Beatrice more instructions about being on her best behavior. Finally, she stood there quietly, with nothing more to say.

"Are we waiting for someone?" I asked, wondering why we didn't just leave. I needn't have bothered because the words were still hanging in the air when Jean-Sébastien rounded the corner and catapulted himself next to me in the rear seat. He hadn't even bothered to open the door.

Show off.

"Jean-Sébastien! That's no way to get into a car," Sister Daphne scolded, though she couldn't hide a little smile.

Why was it that anything Jean-Sébastien did was acceptable, and even adorable? If one of us girls had jumped into the car like that, it would have been considered so improper as to nearly give Sister Daphne a heart attack.

"Where's your sidekick?" I asked not very nicely.

"Staying back in his room. He said he didn't feel well."

I was about to say *good* when Marie turned to look at us. "I thought that was quite manly the way Jean-Sébastien got in the car. Didn't you think so too, Anna Sophia?" She laughed in a weird, girly way.

Oh, gross. Are you flirting *with him?* Marie had to be at least thirty, if not older.

"You are *just* what we need around the castle," Marie went on, giggling some more. "A girl is never too old to have a dashing young man around!" She started the car. "Isn't that right, Anna?"

Ugh. And it's never too early for this girl to throw up, I thought.

I wondered if Lauraleigh would take me home if I told her I was sick.

It might be worth a try. It wouldn't even be a total lie.

Chapter 16

Marie raised the roof of the car and drove like a drunken racecar driver, and we arrived at Irvigne Manor long before Lauraleigh. I hated to admit it, but it looked spectacular. Paper lanterns lined the driveway, and in every window of the enormous house, candles gently flickered.

Inside, everything was set up around a carnival theme. At the end of the parlor, a pair of massive doors opened into a ballroom all decked out with game booths. As I moved closer, I could see attendants standing by games like Whack-a-mole, darts, skee ball, and a ton more I couldn't even name. Every booth had dozens of stuffed toys hanging above for prizes.

"Ooh! Can we go play?" Beatrice asked, her eyes sparkling.

"Of course, dear," Marie said. "Irvigne Manor is all about fun. Now go win yourself a giant teddy bear!"

"Are you coming, Anna?" Beatrice asked, skipping away without waiting for my answer.

I followed her, but more slowly. We were the first guests, and I wanted a chance to see the house before the others arrived.

Candace was busy ordering everyone around, as usual. I hadn't spent a lot of time around her, but it was enough to know I didn't want us to be friends. Like her mother, Candace was just plain bossy. But while Marie might fool some people into thinking she was charming, nobody was fooled into thinking that about Candace. There was nothing charming about her.

"Put that on the table," she yelled to a girl struggling under the weight of an enormous platter. "Not *that* table, the *other* one. And make sure it's straight in the middle!"

Oh, my gosh, it's Mei! I thought, my jaw dropping in horror. Along with Gaëlle and six other girls, Mei had been adopted by the Montmorencys. I had always really enjoyed being around her, but unlike Gaëlle, she hadn't continued as a student at the Collège. I hadn't seen her since her adoption two years earlier — I had assumed she changed schools.

When I first arrived at the orphanage, I had been mesmerized by Mei's delicate bone structure and beautiful almond-shaped eyes. Her hair, always as black and shiny as the keys on a piano, fascinated me. But now, everything about Mei looked dull and wasted way. She didn't look small and delicate now; she looked *emaciated.*

I was too alarmed too speak. But when Mei disappeared down a long hallway and then returned carrying more food, I had recovered enough to know I wanted to talk to her. I wanted to know what was wrong.

"Hi, Mei," I said quietly.

She was so startled she almost dropped the platter of sandwiches she was carrying.

"Oh. Hi, Anna." Her eyes darted across the room to where Candace and Marie were arguing about the music selection, then back to me. "What are you doing here?"

"I got invited. I mean, it's a party, right?"

"Oh. Right." She frowned and turned away, which I found strange. She acted like she wasn't allowed to talk to anyone — like she would get in trouble if she did.

The doors burst open, and a group of guests entered. I didn't recognize any of them. They were adults dressed in fancy clothes with a crowd of laughing children running around them. Gaëlle stood next to Marie, who greeted each guest and then handed Gaëlle their coat. Weighed down under a mountain of coats, Gaëlle hurried into a small room off the parlor. I turned to ask Mei why Gaëlle was doing that, but she was gone.

Music blared throughout the house. It was too loud; it felt intrusive and annoying. Between the music, the noisy people, and the way Gaëlle and Mei were both acting, nothing about Irvigne Manor felt good to me. Nothing at all.

I walked over to Marie and Gaëlle. "Would it be okay if Gaëlle showed me her room? I'd like to put my overnight pack in there."

"Certainly, dear," Marie said with a patronizing smile. "Gaëlle, find Olivia and have her join me here to greet our guests."

"Yes… Mother." Gaëlle lowered her eyes.

I knew Gaëlle well enough to understand she had just choked on using the word *mother*.

I could hardly blame her for that: I'd have choked on it too. It'd be like having to call Cruella de Ville *mother*.

I quickly admonished myself. I didn't have a single good reason to dislike Marie. Just because she rubbed me the wrong way, didn't mean she was a monster. I had to try harder to be nice. I decided I'd spend the rest of the evening channeling good people, like Malala and Anne.

That should help me be nicer, I thought.

"And be sure to give Anna Sophia a tour of our home." Marie's intonations seemed just a bit too chipper. "Let her know exactly what she's missing by hurting our feelings and not letting us adopt her!" She feigned a pout and laughed.

Then again, maybe not.

I might have been slightly unrealistic in setting myself the goal of trying to become as forgiving as Malaya Yousafzai, or as hopeful as Anne Frank. I wasn't sure it was even part of my basic temperament to be either one of those things.

I tried to smile at Marie's pretend joke, so as not to be completely rude. Turning to Gaëlle, I said, "Maybe we should find Beatrice before we go to your room. I don't like the idea of leaving her alone for too long."

I figured I'd work on being a better person later. For the moment, I wanted to make sure Beatrice wasn't by herself in this strange house.

We found her happily tossing bean bags. She was trying to win a stuffed turtle, but she didn't mind stopping for a while — not when it meant getting to see Gaëlle's room.

"Do you have a *fairy* bed?" she asked. "You know, the kind with the lacy top?"

"A canopy bed?" Gaëlle said with a small smile. "As a matter of fact, I do." .

"Is it pink? I love pink." Beatrice began chattering on and on about all her favorite colors, animals, and ice cream flavors. I was glad she, at least, was having a good time.

We crossed the parlor, where the guests were eating canapés and talking loudly. In the corner, a few people had already begun to dance, and some others lounged on couches. I looked around for Lauraleigh but didn't see her.

"Where did all these people come from?" I asked.

"André and Marie know everybody," Gaëlle said with a small shrug. She sounded like she didn't want to talk about it. "The mayor and his family. The chief of police and his family. The principals of all the private schools in Geneva Canton and their families. Et cetera."

I grabbed my backpack from the coatroom and followed Gaëlle toward a massive staircase.

She smiled the first real smile I'd seen from her all night. "Nice backpack," she said. "Monsieur Nolan?"

Until moving out of the orphanage, Gaëlle had plenty of experience with all Monsieur Nolan's bear gifts. I think she loved each one of the bears as much as I did.

"He upped it a notch for my thirteenth." I managed a small laugh. "I thought you'd get a kick out of it."

"I *love* it!" Beatrice practically sang. "When I grow up and turn thirteen, I hope I get one like it!"

"I'll save this one just for you," I told her as we followed Gaëlle up the polished and gleaming stairs. Beatrice squealed with so much excitement at the thought of inheriting the bear pack, I was afraid she'd tumble backwards down the steps. I kept my hand near her back, just in case.

After we had reached the top, we turned and walked down a long hallway. There were beautifully carved doors on each side of it, all closed. As we were about to pass one of them, the door opened, and a small, thin girl came out. She had stringy blonde hair and blue eyes that seemed much too large for her face.

"Marie is looking for you, Olivia," Gaëlle said. "You'd better hurry. You know how she gets."

Olivia bit her lip and nodded before hurrying toward the stairs.

I wondered what Gaëlle had meant by that, and why yet another girl who was supposed to be having a happy life at Irvigne Manor looked so frightened and miserable.

Chapter 17

"Are these all bedrooms for the girls they adopted?" I tried to sound casual. I had so many questions, but I didn't want to ask any of them in front of Beatrice.

"Yes, but only Mei, Olivia, and I are left," Gaëlle replied, averting her eyes. "Everyone else is older now. They've gone off to universities in England, Scotland, and in the States. Or to private boarding schools, you know? It is very generous of André and Marie to offer that to all of us when we reach seventeen."

Her voice sounded like she was reciting something she had memorized: It was flat, and it was weird. I didn't like it.

"They sometimes send us postcards," Gaëlle added. "A lot of happy postcards."

She opened the last door at the end of the hall. Her bedroom was bigger than most of our classrooms back at the Collège. Pale pink wallpaper covered every wall. The fairy bed, as Beatrice had called it, towered like a castle in the middle of the room. Gauzy lace draped over the canopy frame and hung to the floor. At least a dozen pillows were arranged neatly on the satiny, pink bedspread. Beatrice squealed in delight when she saw all the toys and dress-up clothes along one wall and ran off to play with them.

"You can put your pack over here," Gaëlle said, pointing at a velvet love seat. "And the bathroom is through that door."

That old bruise on her face stood out in the bright pink room.

"Thanks." I tore my eyes away from her, still not believing her story about how she'd gotten it, and glanced around the room in wonder. Apart from the mess Beatrice was making, everything was immaculate. It almost appeared to be staged, or like a hotel room no one ever occupied.

"You can't tell me you're happy with this," I said, not even trying to pretend I thought it was great. I knew Gaëlle way too well to believe she'd be comfortable in this kind of room. And she knew me way too well to think it would impress me.

She shrugged. "I don't really spend much time in here."

I couldn't help but wonder where she did spend her time.

Double glass doors led to a balcony. I opened them and stepped into the cool air. The sun was just beginning to set, and flowers in the garden below us glittered in the pale light like jewels. Beyond the garden was the maze of hedges and the brick wall where our balloon had crashed. From above, I could see all the twists and turns of the labyrinth. Oddly, there was a small building in its center.

The labyrinth itself looked intensely confusing, but the building — well, something about it looked terrifying, though for the life of me I couldn't say what. I wanted to look through the dream stone, but Gaëlle was standing right next to me.

"What is that?" I asked, pointing at the building.

Even in the dim light, I saw Gaëlle's face pale. "I don't know," she stammered. "André doesn't let us go into the maze. He says it's too easy to get lost. Come on, let's go inside. I'm cold."

She turned toward the doors, but I stopped her. "Gaëlle, you know I'm your friend, right? You can tell me anything."

She looked me straight in the eye. She was scared; I could see it. But she turned away again and said, "Of course. But I have nothing to tell you. Everything's fine."

Back in her room, we found Beatrice dressed as a fairy princess. Over her dress, she'd added a frilly pink skirt, and on her head, she wore a tall cone hat with a trailing veil.

"Can I wear this when we go back down to the party?" she asked.

Gaëlle smiled. "Of course, you can. How about we make some ice cream sundaes first?"

"Yes!" Beatrice cried out.

I heard voices coming from the far end of the hallway, and a second later, André's thunderous laugh was unmistakable.

"Let me show you our girls' rooms," I heard him say. "This wing is entirely devoted to our daughters. We are so proud of all of them." His booming voice made it clear he was acting as tour guide.

"Let's go this way," Gaëlle said quickly, opening her door and leading us across the hall toward another door.

Before we got there, André spotted us. "Ah! My darling daughter Gaëlle! I see you are with your little friends." He beamed, and he seemed so fake I wanted to slap him.

I seriously need to work on my reactions to these people, I thought. *I'm not at all fair to them.*

It was true: Neither André nor Marie had ever given me a specific reason to react to them like I did. They opened their home to us; Gaëlle had a beautiful room all to herself; she had nice clothes... but I couldn't help it. Something about all of it felt very wrong.

I glanced at Gaëlle.

And then, there's that bruise.

Three people were walking with André. A man and woman dressed in expensive-looking clothes stood on each side of him. A third person, a man, stood apart from them. The couple seemed enthralled by the opulence of the house. The woman touched everything with the tips of her gloved hand. As she touched the walls, the moldings around the door, the side table and lamp, it was as if she couldn't get over how there was not a speck of dust anywhere.

If this is what rich people are like, I thought, *I hope I'm never rich.*

The man standing apart from the others touched nothing, nor did he say anything. He was tall, with long, black hair tied in a neat ponytail that hung down his back. He wore beautifully tailored, black clothing. Everything — his tie, his suit, his shirt, his shoes — was as black as the hair on his head.

He was staring straight at me, and I saw that even his eyes were black.

A smile twitched across his lips. But it wasn't a kind smile. It was a smile that felt as black as the rest of him.

I felt myself shudder as I quickly looked away.

"Who are your daughter's lovely friends?" the man in black asked, and I could feel his eyes still on me. He spoke with a familiar accent, and it took me only a second to realize he sounded like Uncle Misha. He had to be Russian.

Beatrice curtsied and said, "My name is Beatrice. I'm a fairy princess."

"Oh, aren't you *precious!*" the woman gushed as she squeezed Beatrice's cheeks. "I want a little girl just like you." Her husband beamed and nodded.

I wanted to tell her that people can't just go out and *get* a child. She made it sound like getting a daughter was no different than getting a piece of furniture she happened to think was pretty. It infuriated me.

The dark-eyed man never even glanced at Beatrice.

"And your name?" he demanded, his eyes never leaving my face.

"Anna," I said, feeling my heart begin to pound harder for some reason. "Anna Sophia."

I certainly didn't curtsy. I didn't even call him "sir." I stated my name and that was it. I found myself inadvertently clutching at the dream stone around my neck, which had become hot. Very hot.

"You look like a girl I once knew," he said, offering nothing more. It felt creepy, and I remained silent. I did not, however, lower my gaze. I didn't like this man. I especially didn't like that he sounded like my beloved Uncle Misha. But I wasn't about to cower in front of him.

"I… uh… I thought they might like to see the kitchen," Gaëlle said to André. "We were going to go make sundaes."

"Of course, of course, my darling girl!" André said. "You girls need some fattening up. You're all as thin as rakes." He steered his friends back the way they had come.

The man in black watched me over his shoulder as they walked away. A shiver ran down my spine. It was as if his gaze sent a blast of ice in my direction.

I do not like this house. And I most definitely do not like that man.

Chapter 18

Gaëlle pushed the door across the hall. It opened to a second set of steps leading downstairs. Beatrice happily hopped her way down, but I moved slowly. I was thinking about that man and wondering why he'd focused all his attention on me.

The kitchen was bursting with noisy activity.

"Is it okay if we have ice cream?" Gaëlle politely asked one of the cooks. He nodded and waved her away.

Gaëlle walked over to a massive, stainless steel freezer. I couldn't believe how big it was when she opened the door and we could see inside. It contained every kind of ice cream imaginable. Beatrice's eyes opened so wide I thought her eyeballs might fall out of their sockets.

"Better close your mouth before you start drooling," I teased her.

Gaëlle let Beatrice pick out several flavors of ice cream. After setting them all on the counter, she took chocolate sauce and candy sprinkles out of one cabinet, and bowls out of another.

"I used to spend a lot of time here," Gaëlle said with a small smile. "I liked how the cooks were always moving. They never seemed to rest. They used to let me stir the soup sometimes."

"And now?" I asked.

"Now? Well, I'm sure they still never rest. It's just that I'm—" Her eyes did that darting thing again. "Now, I'm just busy with other things, so I don't have time to come down here."

I wanted to ask what other things kept her too busy to visit the kitchen, but there were too many people around, including Beatrice.

I did ask about something else, though. "Those older girls who left to study at the universities and colleges… do they come back here during their holiday?" I don't know why I asked, except something about them being gone was bugging me. I decided to push Gaëlle just a little bit. "Do they call home a lot?"

She seemed caught off guard. "They just, you know — they move on. So, um, no… they don't call or come home because, well, like I said. They just move on." She appeared terribly uncomfortable and wouldn't look at me. "And they send lots of postcards. Marie has albums full of them."

"Don't you find that odd?" I asked. "Doesn't anyone find that odd?"

I was probably trying my luck by asking such a bold question, but I couldn't help myself. Not only did I find it odd, it scared me for Mei and Olivia's sake, and especially for Gaëlle's. Were they going to disappear too?

"Not really," Gaëlle said. "They move on to better lives in different countries, and Marie and André provide them with more money than they'll ever need. Besides, why would anyone care about an orphan's life?"

I stared at Gaëlle. I found her words so strange and unnerving I couldn't help but confront her on it. "Maybe because after they get adopted, they're not *orphans* anymore?"

Instead of responding, she turned to Beatrice. "The ice cream will melt if we don't make our sundaes," she said, faking excitement. "Come on! Aren't you ready for yours?"

Beatrice, of course, was beyond excited to make sundaes. Everyone became very focused on which ice cream went with which sprinkles, and which tasted like the best combination. Gaëlle was overly attentive to everything, except my question about those girls who used to live here.

Beatrice finished her sundae and wanted to play the carnival games again. "But you didn't eat yours!" she said, staring at my full dish.

"I know. I guess I haven't worked up an appetite yet. I'll put it in the freezer, and it will still be ready for eating when I am. How about that?"

"That's good," Beatrice said. "But, Anna? If you're not ready, I might be ready instead."

That made both Gaëlle and me chuckle. "Well, it will be there for you, Beatrice. But remember, if you eat too much, your tummy will hurt."

"I know. Can we play in the carnival room now?" It amazed me how her attention could flit from one thing to the next so quickly.

"We can," I told her. I turned to Gaëlle. "Would you mind taking her there? I need to find the bathroom. I'll come join you when I'm done."

"Sure. It's right through that door." Gaëlle pointed to a door off to my left.

"Great! You two go ahead, and I'll be there soon."

I watched as Beatrice pulled on Gaëlle's hand, tugging her toward the carnival booths. When I was sure they wouldn't look back, I turned to a door on my right.

I tried the door, fully expecting it to be locked, but it wasn't. I decided if anyone saw me, I would pretend I had gotten confused when looking for the bathroom. Taking a deep breath, I opened it just far enough to slip around and close it behind me.

I stepped into a long, dark hallway lit only by one dim bulb. I was pretty sure I had just entered an area *not* on the Montmorency's house tour.

Something bad was going on; I could feel it.

I stood still and listened for any sound suggesting someone was nearby, but I heard nothing. Walking quietly down the hallway,

I came to a staircase leading downward. There were no lights here at all, the steps were narrow, and there was no banister to cling to for guidance. I kept my palm against the wall as I made my way down the steps until I came to a landing.

I stepped down and onto the landing, and the only thing I could see was one small window ahead. Suddenly, that window filled with the light from my moon, illuminating the area. It was like she was offering me the only help she could. And it was plenty; it was enough light for me to see several doors in front of me, all of them closed.

My dream stone grew hot — so hot, it felt like it was burning my skin. I yanked it out from under my shirt and let it dangle, holding its leather thong. It spun clockwise until the leather chain strained; then it spun back the other way. Back and forth it went until, suddenly, it stopped. The moon shone right through the stone's hole onto the keyhole in one of the doors. There was no way this was a coincidence: The dream stone was showing me which of the doors I needed to open.

I wished I had brought Squire with me. He could have scouted things out before I walked through the door alone. Unfortunately, he was in my backpack in Gaëlle's room. I thought about going to get him, but it felt like a huge risk to walk all the way back up the steps, through the dim hallway, into the kitchen, up to Gaëlle's room, and then all the way back to this spot without being seen. It seemed a bigger risk than just walking through the door by myself.

That's what I decided to do. *I am stronger than my fear.*

At least, I could try to be, I thought as I attempted to give myself much needed encouragement.

Oddly, the dream stone wasn't hot anymore — it had gone as cold as ice. I dropped it back under my shirt and shivered as I reached for the door. It wasn't locked, but it was heavy. I could only open it enough to see stone steps traveling further downward into utter blackness. Damp, cold air blew up the stairs, bringing an overpowering stink of decay. Low, pained wails came from below, sending chills up my arms and making the hair rise on every part of my body. They could have been the screams of animals, or… humans. I had no way to tell. Either way, it caused me to instantly recoil from the door.

Everything around me began to spin. I held my stomach and gagged. I had to get out of there.

I need air right now! I need air right this second!

I stumbled back toward the landing and saw a glass door I hadn't even noticed before. I raced toward it, threw open the latch, and ran outside. I heard it slam shut behind me and knew I was probably locked out, but I didn't care. I just needed air.

Crawling toward the bushes at the edge of the patio, I held my stomach as I took deep breaths, trying to steady myself and make the world stop spinning.

Whatever was in that basement felt like living death. It *smelled* like living death. I'd never experienced anything so horrible or horrifying in my life. Whatever was down there — human, animal — was it the thing making Gaëlle, Mei, and Olivia act so frightened?

Are André and Marie keeping some kind of demon or monster down there? Is that what I heard… and smelled? Is that possible?

I shuddered and felt another wave of nausea wash over me.

With shaking hands, I lifted the dream stone and peered at the house through the hole.

And there it was. Again.

Chapter 19

A terrifying blackness oozed around the house. I dropped the stone and wrapped my arms around my stomach. It was like I was trying to protect myself from whatever hideous thing surrounded Irvigne Manor.

I sat beneath the bushes and rocked back and forth, as I tried to figure out what I needed to do. Between the horror I felt inside the house and the fearsome darkness surrounding it, I knew I had to do something. Clutching the dream stone, I felt its comforting weight. This time, it felt neither hot nor cold. It just felt solid and reassuring.

I had to know what was in that basement. If I didn't understand what was in there, I couldn't figure out what to do about it. No matter how scared I felt, I had to go back inside.

I took another minute to breathe, repeating Malala's phrase over and over again. *I am stronger than my fear. I am stronger than my fear. I am stronger—*

I had just started to stand when the back door flung open. André walked out into the patio with another man, and I quickly retreated as far back into the shadows as I could go. No excuse in the world would explain away what I was doing outside, crouched under the bushes.

"You have nothing to worry about," André said. He spoke without his usual bluster. He sounded impatient and even a little worried. "Everything's going according to plan. You'll have all nine, just as I promised."

Nine? Nine what?

The other man didn't speak for a moment. His back was to me, but from where I was hiding, I could see his long, black ponytail. It was the Russian man from upstairs.

"I'm not concerned about quantity," the man said in his accent. "It's the quality of your captives that concerns me."

Captives? I sucked in a breath and pressed myself further into the shrubs. Now I knew for *sure* I couldn't let them find me hiding there.

The two men descended the stairs and walked through the garden.

When I thought they had gone far enough ahead to neither see nor hear me, I crept out from beneath the bushes. I knew I should run far and fast in the opposite direction.

But I didn't do that.

With my heart pounding like a jackhammer, I moved after them. Even though a voice screamed inside my head telling me to get out of there, I followed the two men through the garden and toward the maze of hedges. When they disappeared into it, I hesitated, but only for a second.

I'd seen the labyrinth from above. If I wandered too deeply inside it, I might never find my way out. Nobody would even think to look for me in there. I could die inside the complicated mass of hedges, and no one would even know.

Even worse things could happen: I could stumble right into André and his dangerous friend.

I heard their footsteps echoing as they moved farther away. Despite all the reasons I'd just given myself for not doing it, I slipped through the entrance.

At first, the path was easy to follow. The hedges were neatly trimmed, and the cobblestoned path had been cleared of leaves or stones. I turned the first corner and hurried around the next. I didn't have any choices to make, so I followed the path wherever it led — until I came to a crossroad.

There, I had to make my first choice: right, left, or straight ahead. The men's footsteps seemed to come from all sides. I quieted, trying not to breathe, and soon heard André's voice straight ahead. I followed the sound and continued to move through the maze, listening for their voices and turning around an endless series of corners. I was hurrying along the path, when I almost blundered right into them.

I stopped and crouched low behind the last turn in the hedge. When I peered through some cracks in the hedge, I saw both men standing in front of the small stone building I had seen from Gaëlle's balcony.

The building had no windows and only one iron door, which André opened with an old-fashioned skeleton key. He paused with the door partially open. In the blackness beyond the door, I sensed the same horrifying despair I'd felt coming out from the basement of the house. I was so focused on the pain I sensed coming from the building that I almost missed André's next words.

"We did ask her to join our family." André sounded frustrated. "Several times. I can't force her into adoption. She has some sort of trust fund, so our money seems not to interest her. I can't force her into being legally adopted without raising suspicion. You know that."

"Well, then find another way," the man said, his voice steely and cruel. "She must be part of the Nine, or it's off."

"Sure, sure," André said. "Whatever you want. I understand completely."

My body went cold. Were they talking about me? How many times had I refused André and Marie? At least three. My knees started to tremble, and I fell heavily into the bushes.

"What was that?" the man with the ponytail said, alarmed. "Did you hear that?"

I ran.

My feet skidded around the first turn in the hedge. Footsteps thundered behind me. I couldn't remember every path I'd taken to reach the little building. I rushed around turns blindly, trying to put as much space as possible between myself and the two men chasing me. I had no doubt if they caught me, I would face an unimaginable fate.

I had no time to think. Around a corner, then around another corner. Corner after corner, I just kept running. Then I stubbed my toe on a stone and fell.

"Oomph!" The air whooshed out of my lungs. Laying there, flat on my stomach and trying to breathe, I heard André shout, "This way!"

I got up and blundered around more corners, having no idea where I was going. I only knew I was running faster in my panicked attempt to escape than I had ever run in my life. Tears blurred my vision so much I didn't even see the brick wall until it was inches in front of me. There was no way to stop. I squeezed my eyes shut in anticipation of the collision that would knock me out cold and leave me helpless to defend myself.

But it didn't happen.

Instead of smashing into brick, my bones seemed to liquefy. My body morphed into a single wisp of vapor — as if everything making up who I was collapsed in on itself. Atoms and cells became something other than what they had been, and I felt myself slip through the bricks as if I was doing nothing more than walking through fog.

Only I was the fog this time.

A sudden jolt sent me sprawling across the torn-up grass. This was where our balloon had crashed — except... wait; that meant I was on the other side of the labyrinth! How was that possible? How could I have walked through a brick wall?

I heard André and his friend calling to each other as they searched for me. But of course, they couldn't find me. Not now.

I was on the opposite side of the hedge.

"Did you see where he went?" the man shouted to André.

"He must have turned the other way," André yelled back.

Their voices faded as they moved away.

I sagged in relief and rubbed my ankle, which had started to swell. I must have twisted it when I'd fallen. I was so happy to be out of the labyrinth I didn't even care. I leaned against the wall, which felt solid against my back. I shuddered at the thought of what would have happened if they'd found me — if I hadn't moved through the wall like it was smoke instead of brick.

"What are you doing out here?" The voice startled me enough that I jumped up, ready to run again. But it was only Jean-Sébastien.

"You shouldn't be out here!" I whispered. If André found him, he'd think Jean-Sébastien was the one who had been in the maze.

"I could say the same about you." He raised one eyebrow high.

"I need you to do me a favor," I said, not wanting to get into a sparring match. "I need you to find Lauraleigh and tell her I hurt my ankle and need to go home."

Jean-Sébastien leaned closer to me, concerned. "Are you okay?"

"I just need to go back to the dorm. Will you get Lauraleigh?"

"Sure. Of course," he said. "Can you walk? I can help you."

"I'm okay. Thanks." As he nodded and started to walk away, I stage whispered, "Make sure to get Beatrice too!"

He gave me a thumbs-up and raced back inside the house.

I limped to the front gate to wait for Lauraleigh. All I could think about was how to get Gaëlle and the other girls out of there — how to get them out of there *now.*

I didn't know how much time had passed when Jean-Sébastien's voice sounded behind me again, startling me so badly I nearly passed out.

"Lauraleigh and Beatrice are right behind me," he said. "They'll be here in a second."

"Th—thanks," I stuttered. "Thanks for getting them."

"No problem." He gave me a smile. "You should be careful walking around in the garden by yourself at night."

"You too. You need to be careful here, Jean-Sébastien. Things aren't… They're not what you think."

"What's *that* supposed to mean?" he said with a carefree chuckle. "You're not getting all *Hunger Games* on me, are you?"

"I'm not joking, Jean-Sébastien. I *mean it.*" I rubbed my ankle, which was so swollen it scared me. "I'm serious."

"Okay, *jeez!* I'll be careful." He looked at me as if perplexed. After a second he said, "This is actually a boring party. I think I'll head back with you and Lauraleigh, if that's okay."

It was more than okay. For once, I was happy Jean-Sébastien was staying near me. Who knew what might happen to him if André were to decide he had been the one in the maze.

"You're a strange girl, Anna Sophia," Jean-Sébastien said, narrowing his eyes into slits. "Really strange." He smiled. "Good thing I like strange."

Yeah, well. Liking strange might not be a good thing for you, I thought. *Not when someone's strange because they're a witch.*

I glanced at Jean-Sébastien and smiled, just as Lauraleigh and Beatrice came out.

Part II:
Finding Mei

Chapter 20

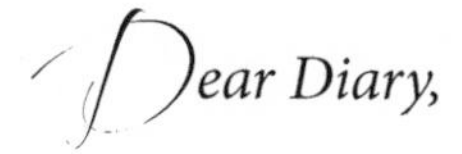*ear Diary,*

I'm having a horribly boring and upsetting weekend.

First, I'll tell you why it's boring.

The biggest reason is I've had to lay around with ice on my ankle for two whole days. I felt terrible lying to Sister Daphne, especially because I knew she'd cluck over me like a mother hen once she saw my swollen ankle. But I couldn't very well say I'd hidden in the maze and walked through a brick wall!

I told her I'd been playing flag football with a group of boys bored with carnival games. Both Sisters believed me, which is good, but then I had to listen to a lecture about how football was a boy's game. And how I needed to be more ladylike and proper. I wanted to remind them that I run faster and throw harder than any of the boys. But my ankle was throbbing, and I had a lump on my forehead, and I just didn't have the energy to argue. I'll debate the merits of equality for girls with them some other time. I know I will have plenty of opportunities, that's for sure.

Now, I'll tell you why this weekend has been so upsetting.

It's because I'm horribly worried about Gaëlle and Mei and Olivia.

I want to know what happened to all those other girls. I don't believe for one minute they're at some fancy university or boarding school. And I'm afraid it's too horrible to even think about where they are.

I must find out what is going on inside Irvigne Manor. Somehow, I need to get back there and look in that basement, and inside the building inside the maze. But how?

There is so much I don't know or understand, Diary. Like, how could I walk through a brick wall? Could I do it again if I wanted? Who is my grandmother and why hasn't she ever let me know she was alive? Why won't Squire tell me about my father?

See? I have so many questions! The worst part is, I don't know a way to find answers. There's no one who can answer them.

I do know one thing though, and it's that something bad is going on at Irvigne Manor. I also know that no matter what, I'm going to find out what it is.

I've been reading Anne Frank's diary this weekend. She wrote, "Despite everything, I believe that people are really good at heart." I don't know how she could have felt that way with all the terrible things happening around her, but she did. I hope she was right. I hope that whatever is going on in Irvigne Manor, it doesn't prove Anne Frank wrong about people.

The weekend was full of parties thrown by graduating students, but I didn't go to any of them. Besides not feeling all that great, it upset me that so many people I cared about were leaving. Especially Lauraleigh.

Lauraleigh was planning to take a gap year to tour Europe. It sounded like a wonderful adventure, and honestly, I was happy for her. It's a great accomplishment to graduate from high school, especially with such high marks. I just had trouble acting excited when I knew it meant she wouldn't be in my life every day. That was selfish, but I had never lied to Lauraleigh about anything — well, apart from why I had the votive candle in my room earlier — and I couldn't lie about being happy she was leaving. She'd know I was lying, just like she knew I'd lied about playing flag football.

After the Sisters had finished lecturing me, Lauraleigh helped me up to my room. As soon as the door was closed, she looked right at me and said, "Do you want to tell me what really happened?"

"I do," I told her. "I desperately want to tell you. You must believe me. But I can't. Not yet." I was near tears. "Are you mad? Is it okay if I don't tell you right now?"

I hated keeping a secret from Lauraleigh, but I just felt like I needed to understand more about being a witch before I could talk about it.

"Sure, it's okay," she said, looking at me kindly. "I'm just worried about you, that's all. Just know anytime you want to talk, I'm here. I'm not going anywhere yet." She gave me a big hug, and as soon as she left my room, I burst into tears.

On Monday, Gaëlle brought my backpack to school. She didn't even ask me why I had left the party in such a hurry, which was weird, but which I also appreciated. I wasn't sure what I would have told her.

As soon as she handed me my bear pack, I tried not to tear it open instantly to check on Squire. On top of everything else I had worried about all weekend, I nearly went out of my mind knowing I had left him alone in Gaëlle's room.

"I'll be leaving next week," she said. She looked nearly ready to cry.

"What do you mean?" I asked as fear filled my gut. "Where are you going?"

"To Scotland. Marie and André have a summer home there." She didn't look happy about that.

"I'm going to miss you." I gave her a hug. I was so afraid where she might *really* be going, I didn't want to stop hugging her. Ever. "I'm so sorry we didn't have our sleepover," I said, finally letting go of her.

"It's probably for the best. You snore." Gaëlle gave me the smallest of smiles.

"I do not!" I said, pretending to be indignant. I felt relieved, seeing even a tiny bit of the old Gaëlle surface. Maybe she would still tell me what was going on over there, after all.

"Well, I have to go," she said. "I just wanted to return your pack. In a couple of hours, Marie will be the keynote speaker at some women's league, and I promised to bring Beatrice along. We're going to be her cheering section."

"Oh, lucky you two." I rolled my eyes. "In case you were just about to invite me, please don't be hurt when I pass."

Gaëlle laughed a sad little laugh. "Don't worry. I already knew you wouldn't go, so I wasn't going to ask."

"Watch out for Beatrice, okay?" I shuddered at the thought of her spending more time with Marie. Beatrice couldn't see past the canopy bed and the toys to recognize all the sadness in Gaëlle's eyes. She had always wanted a new family, and the Montmorencys made sure they were a tough act for any kid to turn down.

After Gaëlle had left, I strolled through the courtyard to get some fresh air. I also wanted to be alone to think about something brewing inside my head. I wished I had asked Gaëlle if André was also going to be part of the cheering section for Marie. I'd walked through a brick wall once. Hopefully, I could do it again — because the idea bubbling in my head was that getting myself inside Irvigne Manor would involve walking through a wall.

I knew I at least had to try.

First, I needed to figure out how to get there and how to return before curfew. Things were more relaxed during the summer break, but they were not so relaxed I could sneak in after curfew and not get into big trouble.

I knew I could ask Lauraleigh, but then she'd have to tell Sister Constance where we were going. She would never lie about something like that. Plus, if I told her *why* I wanted to go there, she'd insist on telling Sister Constance right away. Until I had real proof, I was positive it would be a mistake to share my suspicions with anyone. On top of all that, Lauraleigh just wasn't the snooping-around type. It would be horribly uncomfortable for her.

No, for once, Lauraleigh was not the one who could help me.

But if not her, then who? I couldn't very well walk all the way to Irvigne Manor, and I sure couldn't fly. Not yet, anyway.

Then, just like that, I knew. *Jean-Sébastien!*

Jean-Sébastien was always coming up with schemes to make money. During the past two summers, he had weeded gardens and trimmed bushes for some of the orphanage's wealthy neighbors. In winter, he had shoveled their walkways. And in autumn, he'd raked and bagged their leaves. Between all those things, he'd saved enough money to buy a small motorbike. One that could easily carry two people all the way to Irvigne Manor.

It'd be so much easier to ask this of him if he owed me a favor, but he didn't. Actually, I probably owed him one for helping me out with my hurt ankle. It didn't matter, though, because I was still going to ask him to take me to Irvigne Manor.

I knew one other thing about Jean-Sébastien — he was always up for an adventure. I hoped that would convince him to take me. Because, for sure, sneaking into Irvigne Manor was bound to be an adventure.

I only hoped it wouldn't be a bad one.

Chapter 21

I found Jean-Sébastien cleaning his motorbike in the small garage behind the orphanage. A pail of soapy water sat beside him as he wiped down the tire rims with a wet cloth.

"Hey," I said, trying to sound casual. No need to let on how desperate I was for his help.

He glanced at me over his shoulder. "Hey. How's your ankle?"

"Practically as good as new. Although I might not be quite ready to race you yet."

He snorted. "Like you'd ever have a chance of beating me." He dipped his rag in his bucket and made a show of wringing it out. "What do you want, Anna Sophia?"

"Why do I have to want something? Maybe I just wandered over to say hello and see your motorbike."

He half-turned to me and rolled his eyes. "Right. And pigs wear lipstick during the summer. You've *never* wandered over here for no reason. So, what's up? I know you need something."

Ouch. That made me feel bad. Thankfully, not so bad that I wouldn't still ask for his help.

"Does Mei go to your school?" I asked. "I'm not changing the subject. Mei is part of why I'm here."

Jean-Sébastien attended the only high school besides the Collège that sat between the orphanage and the Montmorencys castle. Since Mei hadn't been back to the Collège after she was adopted, I assumed that if she was going to school at all, it had to be Jean-Sébastien's.

"Mei?" he asked, looking up from his bike. His brownish-blond hair fell into his eyes, and he brushed it away with a soapy hand. For some extremely odd reason, I found it to be a sweet gesture.

"You must remember her," I said, happy to change the focus of my attention. "She used to live in the orphanage. André and Marie adopted her a couple of years ago. I thought she might go to your school."

"Oh, right. *Mei*. Yeah, I remember her, but no — she doesn't go to my school. If she did, I'd have seen her. It's not that big. Maybe they're homeschooling her or something. Why?"

I shifted from foot to foot, unsure of how much to say. "Don't you think it's odd she isn't in school? I don't really see Marie and André as the type to be devoted homeschool parents."

"Maybe they sent her to a boarding school."

"Huh uh. I saw her at the party last Friday. You didn't see her there?"

Jean-Sébastien stood up and frowned. "No. Why?"

"I don't know. It's just that… she seemed unhappy and really, really stressed. She didn't look well to me. She was thin and pale—"

"Meaning what? You think they're keeping her locked up in a room like Rapunzel?" Jean-Sébastien gave a little snort of laughter as he wiped his hands on the cloth and threw it in the pail.

"No, I just—"

For the first time, I noticed a bit of fuzz on Jean-Sébastien's upper lip. I was so taken aback by even noticing this, I immediately felt embarrassed and confused. I stopped talking right in the middle of my sentence, and without even thinking about it, I moved a couple of meters away from him. And then, for some reason, I started acting like I was mad, even though I wasn't.

"Never mind. *Just forget it,*" I said. "It's no big deal."

He stared at me, arching an eyebrow.

"*What*?" I snapped. "I mean it. Sorry I bothered you."

Jean-Sébastien continued to stare at me without saying anything. He looped his thumbs over the pockets of his shorts and leaned against the edge of his motorbike seat. He looked like he was in a TV commercial or something. "I don't remember saying you were bothering me."

When did he get so cute?

This wasn't at all what I expected when I had wandered over there. It had all become too maddening and confusing, and I didn't even know what to say at that point. So I didn't say anything. I just stood there feeling like an idiot.

"Looks like something is bothering *you,* though," Jean-Sébastien said casually. "You might as well spill what it is, since you'll tell me eventually, anyway."

"Okay. *Fine,*" I said, totally exasperated. "I *am* bothered, you're right about that. I'm bothered because something weird, something *bad* is going on at Irvigne Manor. And… and I must get over there to check it out, so I know if Mei and Gaëlle are okay, and I need to see what is going on because I know they're not, and I know something horrible is happening, but I don't know what, and the only way I can find out is if you take me there on your motorbike."

I said this whole thing in a rush of words without so much as pausing for breath.

"Weird and bad — how?" he asked, completely ignoring the part about needing him to take me there.

"Weird like, Gaëlle walks around like she's a ghost most of the time, and she won't talk to me about it even though she used to talk to me about everything. And weird like, she has a bruise on her eye and I know she's lying about how she got it. And weird like, Marie and André making a huge deal over how much they love being parents, but during the party Marie treated Mei and Gaëlle more like servants than daughters. There's another girl who lives there, too: Olivia. They treated her the same way." Once I started, the words came pouring out of me. I took a quick breath.

"There's other stuff, Jean-Sébastien. *Bad* stuff. Except, I'm not going to tell you what it is. Not yet, anyway. Not until I at least know if you're in or out. If you're out, that's just fine because I'm going to find out what's going on over there, whether you help me or not."

I folded my arms and glared at him.

One side of Jean-Sébastien's mouth tugged up at the corner, making him look semi- amused. "Whoa! Settle down, girl. Who knew you could get so riled up!"

He was teasing me. I could tell, because his eyes were smiling — not in a mocking way, but in a kind way. It surprised me, although it shouldn't have. When I thought about it, Jean-Sébastien had never been anything *but* nice. A little wild, maybe, but nice.

"This all sounds very creepy," he said. "I'm definitely in." Before I could say anything, he put his hand up, adding, "On one condition."

"What?"

"You tell me what you mean by *bad* stuff. If I'm in, I have the right to know what I'm getting myself tangled up in."

I hesitated, but then realized he was right. It wasn't fair to ask him to help me and not tell him why. I didn't need to tell him *everything*, but I needed to tell him enough so he could decide if he still wanted to be involved.

"Okay." I looked at him, trying to gauge what I could safely disclose. "So, you know when I hurt my ankle the other night?"

He nodded.

"I hurt it in the maze."

His eyebrows shot up in surprise.

"There was a weird guy there with André. *Creepy*-weird, Jean-Sébastien. He spoke with a Russian accent and had a long black ponytail."

"I saw that dude. He was dressed all in black, right?"

"Right. And the thing was, I had this bad feeling about — well, about everything. Which is why I followed them into the maze—"

"Wait. You followed them into that labyrinth thing?"

"Yes. But then I fell into the bushes, and they heard me. I was running like a crazy person because they were chasing me—"

Jean-Sébastien let out a low whistle. "Did they know that was you?"

"No! They didn't see me, because I got out of the maze before they did. But that's why, when you found me, I was glad you let Lauraleigh bring you back. I was afraid if they saw you, they would think it was *you* in there because I know they thought I was a boy. Or a man. I mean, I heard them refer to me as a 'he.'" I took a deep breath. Just telling Jean-Sébastien about that night felt stressful.

He nodded, encouraging me to continue.

"There's a building inside the maze, and I don't know what's inside it. I think it might be something awful. Really awful,

Jean-Sébastien. But I don't want to say anything to Sister Constance, or to anyone until I know if I'm right or just being stupid."

"And you want me to take you over there to check it out?"

"Yep."

Jean-Sébastien shook his head, a look of amazement on his face. "You're not just strange, Anna Sophia. You're *crazy.*"

I looked at him in surprise. Did that mean he wouldn't take me?

He laughed. "All I can say is, I must like crazy because I'm in."

I let out one big, whooshing breath I didn't even know I had been holding. It was all I could do not to hug him. Not that I would hug him. I wouldn't. I mean, I couldn't, of course, because—

"When do you want to do this?" Jean-Sébastien asked, interrupting a series of very embarrassing thoughts crowding inside my head.

"*Now!*" I cried out, too fast and too loud. I took another breath and said, a little more calmly, "It has to be now because I'm pretty sure everyone will be gone. Marie is speaking at some function, and I know Gaëlle is going with her. I'm hoping André is, as well. Mei and Olivia will probably be home, and I think they'll be in their rooms."

"Let's go, then." He started to roll his motorbike out of the garage.

"Wait. I must go to my room and get my pack. It'll just take a minute."

"Okay, but you'd better make it fast if we're going to snoop around and still get back before curfew. Grab your pack and meet me at the back gate."

"Okay. Thank you so much, Jean-Sébastien. *Really!*"

"Yep." He kicked up the stand of the bike, hopped on, and started the engine practically in one fell swoop. "See you at the gate, Sherrill Holmes," he said, and drove out the garage toward his dorm.

I didn't even get it until I was halfway to my room. *Sherrill* Holmes. Like Sherlock Holmes, only a girl. Funny.

Who knew Jean-Sébastien had a sense of humor.

Sherrill Holmes. It made me chuckle, even in my stressed state of mind.

It also made me feel weird.

But in a nice way, even if it *was* confusing.

Chapter 22

ear Diary,

I have only a minute to write before I head out, so I'll be brief.

I'm so relieved Jean-Sébastien is taking me to Irvigne Manor. As I'm getting ready to go, I can't help but think about something Sister Mary Agnes read to us by Malala Yousafzai. It was, "When the whole world is silent, even one voice becomes powerful."

It seems to me everyone has been silent about all those girls disappearing. And Gaëlle has been silent about what is happening to her. And now I think I might be about to find out what's really going on at Irvigne Manor. And if I find out I'm right about something bad happening there, I promise you this, Diary: I will make my one voice powerful.

I will make my voice even more powerful than my magic. I will have to, if Mei and Gaëlle and those other girls are going to survive.

I'm really, really scared, but I'm still going.

Jean-Sébastien is waiting, so I will have to write you more later.

Wish me luck!

I ran to my room and grabbed my backpack, tossing Squire, a candle, and a pack of matches in it. At the last second, I threw in a pen and some paper. I didn't plan to tell Jean-Sébastien about Squire, but just in case I needed him, I wanted a way for us to communicate.

I hoped I wouldn't see the Sisters on my way out. Even during our summer break, we were not allowed to leave campus without permission. I could only hope I didn't get caught. Leaving was bad enough; leaving with a boy would be way worse. Even if it was only Jean-Sébastien.

When I reached the gate, I was out of breath from running, and my ankle throbbed with dull pain.

Jean-Sébastien sat on his motorbike, waiting for me. When I was close enough, he tossed me an extra helmet.

"Thanks!" I said. I was touched he thought about my safety. It made me feel a little giddy, to be perfectly honest. I'm not usually a giddy kind of girl, so that *definitely* felt strange.

"It may be too big for you," he said. "But it's better than nothing."

Once I had it on, he leaned over to me and pulled the chin strap tight. To my surprise, I felt my stomach flutter. His face was so close to mine I could practically count his eyelashes. Which, I noticed, were longer than mine.

What is going on with me? This is crazy!

Stupid was more like it.

"Hop on and hold on," Jean-Sébastien said before I could spend any more time thinking about my reactions and acting even weirder than I already was.

Doing as directed, I hopped on. I felt like a total dork, straddling the seat and wrapping my arms around his waist. It felt so awkward I thought I might die of embarrassment, and I was just about ready to let go when the bike took off. I swear, we went from zero to a hundred in two seconds flat. At that point, there was nothing awkward about wrapping my arms around him because I wasn't just holding on — I was gripping him so hard I'm surprised I didn't cut off his air supply.

Once we had been going for a few minutes, I began to relax my death grip and enjoy the scenery. What an amazing feeling it was to zoom down the coastal road on a motorbike and see Lake Geneva shimmering under the afternoon sun. I could see sailboats in the distance, wind surfers closer in, and the Alps towering over it all. It was so beautiful it took my breath away.

Everything seemed so much closer than from the inside of a car, and all my senses sprang alive at once. It felt like we were going so fast that at any minute we would take off flying, although I'm sure we weren't going nearly as fast as when I've traveled the same road in a car. Sitting behind Jean-Sébastien, I felt every bump in the road. Yet it was exhilarating and electrifying, and I couldn't stop smiling. Although after a bug flew in my mouth and I nearly choked on it, I learned that smiling on a motorbike was better done with a closed mouth.

When the road dipped closer to the lake, the mossy, earthy smell of trees and beach combined to nearly send me into oblivion. A second later we were past it, and the booming sound of the wind took over my senses.

If the Sisters could see me, they'd probably ground me for life — right after drowning me in lectures about the dangers of riding on such a contraption. That was what Sister Constance would call the motorbike — a *contraption.* They'd probably make sure the head of Jean-Sébastien's dorm grounded him from ever riding it again, or at least until after he graduated from high school.

It would be *so* bad if they saw me, so I had no intention of the Sisters ever finding out about me riding that motorbike. It was the best experience of my life so far, and there was no way I'd let them take it away from me. It didn't even matter I was only here right now because of the terrible things happening at Irvigne Manor. I was on a motorbike with the wind in my face and my hair blowing behind me, and loving every second of it!

On top of everything else, it made me feel grown up. I liked that feeling, too.

Jean-Sébastien said something over his shoulder, but the wind whipped away his words. I figured it couldn't have been too important. He was probably just pointing out the beauty of the setting sun as we turned west towards the hills and Irvigne Manor. Or maybe he was trying to tell me we were about to tackle a series of steep switchbacks that would probably scare a few years of life out of me. Which they did, but I survived. Somehow, going up the steep mountain road in a car didn't feel anywhere near as thrilling or dangerous as it did on the motorbike.

After the last switchback, I noticed our speed decreasing as Jean-Sébastien pulled over to a dip in the road and stopped. Taking off his helmet, he turned to me. "In case someone is there, we don't want them to hear the motor. Hop off, and I'll stash the bike in those bushes. We can walk the rest of the way."

I was impressed. He clearly had more snooping experience than I did. I'd never have thought of that.

Once we were both off the bike, Jean-Sébastien wheeled it over to the bushes and slid it among them until it wasn't visible from the road. He placed both helmets on the bike, and said, "Let's go!"

To my surprise, he didn't head back to the road but started walking through the forest. Of course, this made sense. It was just another thing I wouldn't have thought of on my own.

It occurred to me, if I planned to keep doing this sort of thing, I might need to improve my Sherlock Holmes skills. Or, *Sherrill* Holmes skills, as it were.

The sun hadn't yet sunk below the mountains, but the forest was already full of shadows. We followed a narrow animal path that appeared to lead in the general direction of the Manor. The trees in this part of the forest were not like those surrounding Bear Paw Boulder. Back there, they were massive in size, and when I walked through them, it was like walking through a dense and magical wonderland. These trees, however, were thin, with none of the peace or grandeur of the Bear Paw Boulder trees. These seemed young, and they let in a lot of light, allowing the undergrowth to flourish. There must have been a fire not so very long ago, because we were walking through the kind of regrowth that occurs after complete devastation. So many plants and flowers budded all around, I didn't even know the names for half of them. Between listening to all the birds tweeting and singing, and looking at the new growth, I didn't realize how close we were to Irvigne Manor until we got there.

We emerged from the trees, and I saw that the labyrinth stood between the Manor and us. I motioned to Jean-Sébastien to follow me. Staying within the protection of the trees, we moved closer to the house until I gestured for us to stop.

We watched the silent house for several long minutes. From where we stood, we just couldn't tell very much about anything that might be going on inside.

"What are we looking for?" Jean-Sébastien whispered.

"I want to make sure André is gone, and then I want to find Mei and make sure she's okay," I whispered back. "Then I want to go inside the maze."

Jean-Sébastien raised his eyebrows and nodded. I liked that he didn't try to take over and seemed comfortable with following my plan. Not that I had much of a plan, because even if I wanted to try walking through the walls to get inside Irvigne Manor, I obviously couldn't do it in front of him. I wasn't even sure if I could do it again in the first place.

"Let's keep to the trees and work our way to the front of the house. Maybe from there, we'll be able to tell if André is home." I hoped a better plan would come to me as we got closer, but I wasn't all that optimistic.

Once there, all we could tell was that Marie's car was gone. André's car wasn't in front of the house, but that didn't mean anything. It could be in one of the garages that housed half a dozen of their fancy cars. The windows of the house were all dark, so it was impossible to tell if he was inside or not.

"Looks pretty quiet in there," Jean-Sébastien said. "How were you planning to get inside? I assume they have a security system in place."

"I hadn't thought about that." I felt like an idiot. Did I think we could just break into their house and not get caught? If I got arrested for breaking and entering, not only would it ruin the rest of my life, nobody would believe me about the bad things happening inside. Everybody in town thought André and Marie were the perfect couple — and the perfect parents. The perfect everything. It was only I who seemed to think differently.

We stood hidden in the trees, neither of us saying anything.

"Come on," I said. "I have an idea."

Without waiting for Jean-Sébastien to ask what it was, I took off and headed in the direction of the labyrinth.

"Anna, *wait*."

When he caught up to me, he said, "Are you going to the maze?"

"Yes," I said. "I think that building I told you about connects to the house."

"Do you *know* it connects to the house? Or do you just think it *might* connect to the house?"

"Well—" I said, drawing out the word to buy time to think of a good answer. "I think it does. The only way to know for sure is to go inside and find out." With that, I started walking toward the labyrinth as fast as my ankle would let me. I was glad it had at least stopped throbbing because I wasn't about to slow down.

"Come if you want," I said over my shoulder. "But if you're too chicken, that's fine. I'll go by myself."

I hoped that was enough bait to make Jean-Sébastien follow me. No *way* did I want to go in there alone.

He whispered something I couldn't hear, but followed.

Chapter 23

When we reached the maze, I closed my eyes for a minute and tried to remember the turns I had taken before.

"Anna," Jean-Sébastien said quietly. "We don't have to do this. If we get lost in there, we have no way to find our way out."

"We won't get lost. I did this before, remember?" I said that with way more confidence than I felt, but I also knew we had to do this. It was our only chance to get into the house and find Mei and Olivia.

Once inside the hedges, I didn't hesitate. Like the last time, the going was easy at first. When we'd reached the first crossroad, I remembered to go straight, and I remembered the next two turns as well. Just when I was feeling confident I was leading us in the right direction, we hit a dead end.

"Oh," I said. "Whoops."

We retraced our steps. When we got to the spot where we had to choose right or left, I felt the dream stone start to vibrate against my chest. I turned left, and nothing happened to the stone, but when I took the next left, it practically jumped out of my shirt. When I turned right instead, it went back to a gentle hum.

Hoping Jean-Sébastien couldn't see the unusual movement around my neck, I let the dream stone lead us toward the building. If I chose the correct turn, it thrummed quietly. If I chose wrong, it quickly let me know. I felt lucky Uncle Misha had given me this amazing and helpful gift, and I silently thanked him. I hoped that, somehow, he felt my gratitude.

All along, I knew that if we *did* get lost in the maze, we'd still be okay. Even though it would probably freak out Jean-Sébastien, if I had to, I would wake up Squire so he could guide us where we needed to go. I was glad that, so far, I hadn't had to do that. I trusted Jean-Sébastien; I wouldn't have told him my worries about Irvigne Manor if I didn't. That said, I wasn't sure I trusted him enough to introduce him to my animated, pen-wielding hand.

We came to the hedge I immediately recognized as the one I'd crushed when I fell. I could see where some of the leaves were still flattened. As soon as we rounded the corner, just as I knew we would, we saw the building.

"*Whoa,*" Jean-Sébastien said as he stared at the big, iron door. "This thing looks… kinda foreboding."

"I know. I told you it was really creepy."

"That's kind of like saying *The Ring* is a little bit of a scary movie, Anna." He shoved his hands deep into his pockets.

We both stood for a minute, staring at the door. A sudden noise made me back away. "Did you hear that?" I asked sharply.

"What?" Jean-Sébastien said, whipping his head around.

"I thought I heard footsteps. Will you do me a favor? Go around the corner and stand guard while I try to get inside. Let me know if you see or hear anybody. And I'll let you know if I get in."

Jean-Sébastien nodded and hurried around the corner. I wasn't worried about the fact there was no place to run, should Jean-Sébastien see someone. The noise that I had heard was probably just a bird, and I just made up hearing footsteps. I didn't need an audience for what I was about to do.

I tried the door handle, but it was locked, which I'd expected. I had seen André use a key, and I had no reason to believe he hadn't locked the door when they'd left.

I knew what I had to do — I just hoped I could do it. I had no doubt an iron door was way denser than a brick wall.

Clutching my dream stone, I closed my eyes. I imagined myself as fluid as mist rolling through the forest at dawn. I pictured every cell, every atom, every molecule, and every vein and bone in my body turning into nothing more solid than a whispered breath. As I inched forward, I willed myself to slip through the door with no more effort than air drifts through clouds on a summer day.

I am vapor; I am the morning fog; I am smoke...

It had to work. I had no other choice.

I am stardust; I am air; I am—

An icy blast of air shot through me like an arrow. I jerked violently and fell on top of a solid stone floor.

I gulped in a breath and stretched out limbs I couldn't see in the pitch-black space. *I did it! I walked through a solid iron door!*

As far as I could tell, I was still in one piece. But the sick smell that wafted from somewhere nearby made me jump to my feet. *Jean-Sébastien!* I needed to find the door and let him in.

I couldn't see the fingers I held in front of my eyes. It was a blackness like I'd never known, and it terrified me. My heart pounded so hard it felt like my chest was about to burst wide open as I felt along the wall in search of the door.

Finally, my fingers stumbled over what felt like a handle of some kind. It was so heavy I could barely turn it, even using two hands. A feeling of panic rose like bile, and I had to force myself to breathe and keep trying. After what seemed like forever, it twisted to the right, and the door opened.

I called out to Jean-Sébastien as loud as I dared, and saw him dart around the corner.

"We're in." I pulled on his hand before he could ask me any questions. "Come on, I think there's a tunnel, or passageway connecting this to the house."

After he walked in through the door, I said, "Hold on. Don't close the door for a second. It's freaky dark when it's closed." I unzipped my pack and pulled out the candle and matches. "No way are we going without this."

I lit the candle and prayed it would keep us from being sealed inside there in utter blackness. It didn't give off a lot of light, but it gave at least *some* light. In between the dancing shadows it created, we could see a narrow tunnel leading downward.

"Holy... bleep!" Jean-Sébastien said, probably avoiding a stronger word only on my account. "What is that *stink?*" He pulled the collar of his t-shirt over his nose. "Man, that is *foul,* Anna. That is bad."

"I know." I used the sleeve of my own t-shirt to cover my nose. "The part I forgot to tell you is that before I went into the maze, I snuck into an area André and Marie don't include on their grand tour. This same smell was coming from the basement in that part of the house. That's why I'm sure this tunnel connects us.

"You sure got around last Friday," Jean-Sébastien said, his voice muffled.

We walked in silence after that. The floor, paved with damp flagstones, felt cold. The brick walls were worn smooth with age. Metal sconces appeared at regular intervals, but they had no torches in them. The tunnel never turned. It was one straight path, sloping ever downward and into the ground. The air felt thinner, and I couldn't stop thinking we were inside an underground tomb.

What if once people go down there, they can't get out? What if that smell is all the dead people who ended up buried alive down there?

It was easy to work myself up into a frenzy as we kept walking downward, and the terrible odor of rot got progressively stronger.

I told myself to get a grip. I reminded myself André and the awful man had been headed inside this building when I'd alerted them to my presence. They wouldn't have been going inside if they had no other way to get out.

Finally, we came to a second iron door which was thankfully open, although it was barely ajar. The hinges had rusted solid, and even using our combined strength, we couldn't push it open any further.

"We'll have to squeeze through," I whispered.

Before either one of us moved so much as one step, a horrifying wail bounced off the walls and echoed back to wherever it originated.

Jean-Sébastien jumped nearly half a meter into the air. "What the—" he whispered. "What was *that*?"

"I don't know," I responded, every hair on my head standing on end. "But I think we're about to find out."

Chapter 24

Squeezing ourselves through the narrow opening was no small feat, but somehow, we both managed to do it. I was so scared I'd get stuck I practically had a panic attack. But there was no time to dwell on my anxieties; and on this side of the door, I could see dim light ahead.

As soon as we crossed through the narrow opening, another round of agonized wailing pierced the air.

"That was *human*, Anna," Jean-Sébastien said. He was so pale he looked like a ghost. "We need to help whoever that is… *now*." He moved forward rapidly.

"Wait! Did you hear that?" I stopped to listen. It wasn't the awful wailing I heard this time. It was quieter. It was a girl's voice, and she was crying. Hearing someone cry like that was even worse. It sounded more personal, and *so* much sadder than even the agonized wailing. It broke my heart.

"Come on," Jean-Sébastien said gently. "We're getting close. Are you okay?"

I nodded and took a deep breath before we continued to walk down the tunnel. Up ahead, we could see it curve to the left.

After we rounded the corner, the tunnel ended and we found ourselves standing at the edge of a large, rectangular room. One dim bulb dangled from the ceiling, providing the only light available. It cast shadows in every direction, hiding and distorting parts of the room. As our eyes started to adjust, both of us gasped when our brains processed what we saw. My hands flew to my mouth. Almost instinctively, Jean-Sébastien moved as close to me as he could get. He was so close I could feel him shaking. I wasn't sure if he was trying to protect me or comfort himself, or both. It didn't matter. Either way, I was glad he was there.

It felt like we had walked onto the set of a horror movie. Walls made of cement blocks insulated only the sound but offered no protection against the chill. The air was thick and stuffy. Even wearing shoes, I could feel the cold coming off the cement floors. Six small, barred cells occupied one side of the room, and three steel doors lined up the other. Each door had a small window with six narrow metal bars, instead of glass.

The stench here was horrendous. It was a mix of sweat, excrement, and rotten food. I only hoped it was not also the stench of death. Whatever terrors I had imagined happening in Irvigne Manor, not one of them came even close to being as dreadful as what we were seeing.

In the middle of the room stood a massive device — an old, beaten up wooden chair with ropes and pulleys surrounding it. It looked like an antique torture machine. As I stared at it, speechless, I felt the dream stone become burning hot against my chest. I tore my eyes off that chair and put the stone on the outside of my shirt.

When we entered the room, we could tell at least one person was in there somewhere. It was obvious they were trying not to make noise, but the sound of intermittent sobs was unmistakable. Somewhere in there was a girl, and we needed to find her.

"Hel—hello?" I called out tentatively.

When there was no response, Jean-Sébastien said, "Please. Tell us where you are. We're here to help you."

Silence filled the room.

Jean-Sébastien motioned to the door at the far end of the wall. We walked toward it, and because he was tall enough to look through the barred window and I was not, that's what he did. He shook his head and walked to the middle door. Again, he looked and saw nothing.

I handed him the candle, and he held it up to the window of the third door. He reeled back, dropping it. My stomach tensed, and I felt like I couldn't breathe.

"Wh—what's in there?" I stuttered, terrified of what he was going to say.

I saw a tear glinting in the corner of his eye. His voice caught as he said the one word I was most afraid to hear. "*Mei*," he whispered. "It's Mei."

I jumped up on my toes and pulled on the bars so I could look in. "Mei! Mei! It's me. It's Anna Sophia. And Jean-Sébastien. We're here. We're here to help you."

I heard a shuffling sound, and a second later Mei's dirt-smeared face peered at me through the bars.

"You can't be here," she whispered, obviously petrified. "They'll find you. You must leave. You must leave *now*, Anna." She stopped talking as tormented sobs racked her body.

I glanced back at Jean-Sébastien. His face was deathly white in the flickering light.

"You'll leave with us," I said. "We came here to find you."

"I'm going to see where those stairs lead," Jean-Sébastien whispered. "Maybe I can find a key to the door."

I nodded and turned back to Mei. A frightful thought struck me. The man with the ponytail said there had to be nine captives. This room had exactly nine cells. I knew nobody was behind the other two solid doors, but—

Bolting across the room, I ran from cell to cell. Small, intimidated figures huddled in the corner of each one. When I came to the last one, Olivia stared at me with wide, terrified eyes. She put a trembling finger to her lips and said, "Shh!"

My whole body shook. I could hardly think as I raced back to Mei.

"What is this?" I asked, beyond myself with worry and fear. I struggled to believe what I was seeing was real. "Tell me what you can, Mei. Tell me so we know how to help you. *Please.*"

Between agonizing sobs, Mel explained how the Montmorencys used adoption as a front for some activity, although she didn't know what. She only knew they told everyone the girls were off studying at expensive, foreign universities, but they most likely weren't. Mei said she didn't know what happened to them, and she had no proof of anything. She only knew once they left the Manor, most were never heard from again — and because the Montmorencys had become such pillars of the local society, no one had ever investigated the fates of the young girls.

No wonder Gaëlle avoided answering my questions, I thought. *Those poor people! All those girls... gone.* I wondered if they would ever be found. If they *could* be found.

"Two years ago, they adopted me so I could be their poster child," Mei said, her voice saddled by tears. "I was going to be their token Asian daughter — the one they were so *gracious* to take into their family and show off at all their fancy balls so everyone could think what wonderful people they are." She paused and wiped her nose on her sleeve.

It was silent for a moment, and I thought, *Mei's not any taller than I am. She must be standing on a box or something. I had to haul myself up by the bars to see in there.* I wondered if they provided it so she could see out when they put someone in the chair. The thought of such unspeakable cruelty made me shudder in horror.

Mei started speaking again, and I turned my attention back to what she was saying.

"I couldn't do it. They scared me so much, Anna. Marie said I always looked afraid of her, which I was, so I don't know how I was supposed to look any other way. They started beating me and keeping me down here. Except, of course, when they need me to be on public display like last Friday. Now they take Gaëlle to the parties, but she'll be replaced when they find a better poster child… like Beatrice." She burst into tears again.

Beatrice!

"Gaëlle and Beatrice are with them tonight," I said, every part of me feeling ill.

"I know." Mei wiped her nose again. "They're grooming her, Anna. To replace Gaëlle. Every day they bring Gaëlle down here and show her the empty cell next to mine. André told her she isn't looking perky enough. He said if she doesn't start acting happier and more grateful, this will be where she gets to live. Up until now, they've let her stay upstairs and go to school. But it's in exchange for pretending she loves this place, and that we're all one big happy family. *Right.* One great big happy family." More sobs accompanied her words.

"Why doesn't Gaëlle tell the police? Or someone in school? Or anyone?" I demanded.

Mei disappeared from view, then popped back up again. "Don't you understand?" she whispered. "If she does it, at least one of us here will die. She's… she is protecting us."

I thought of Gaëlle's vacant eyes when she had told me she was going away for the summer. *Is this what she really meant — that she was going to be hidden away down here?*

Mei pushed her fingers out through the bars toward me. "You have to help us, Anna! We're running out of time. Something big is going to happen. They keep saying when they have nine of us, we'll be shipped off. Without waiting till we turn seventeen. I don't know where we're going, but I know it's going to be even worse than it is here!"

"When they have nine?" A feeling of dread washed over me.

Mei shook her head. Tears mixed with the dirt on her face and I saw that she was shivering.

"Those kids over there and I make seven." A sob caught in Mei's chest. "Gaëlle makes eight. They'll keep Beatrice here for show, and because she's young, they won't send her away for a few years. But by then, they will have ruined her."

I could only stare at her.

"I heard André talking to the Black Horseman," she whispered, her eyes growing huge. "They have their ninth girl, but something is holding them up. I don't know what it is, but when they figure it out, it's over."

I'm the something holding them up, I thought, feeling like I was going to vomit. I was the only thing standing between here and wherever they were going to send everyone.

"What's the Black Horseman?" I asked.

"No." Mei shook her head. "Not what. *Who.* He's that horrible man with the black ponytail."

Jean-Sébastien stumbled down the stairs, taking them two at a time and interrupting anything else Mei had to say. He looked out of breath.

"Okay," he said. "There's a guard's room halfway up this staircase. A guard is sitting inside, but he's sound asleep. The problem is — the keys are on his belt, and there's no way I could get them without waking him up."

I stood on my tip toes and reached through the bars to give Mei's fingers a squeeze. "Listen to me, Mei. We'll be back for you. I promise you. We will be back to get you out of here."

Mei nodded through her tears. "Be careful," she said.

As I started to walk away, Mei called out my name in such an anguished tone, it stopped me cold. I turned and walked back toward her.

"Beware of him, Anna. The Black Horseman. He's very bad," she whispered. "He's very, very bad, Anna."

I nodded. Somehow, I already knew this.

Chapter 25

Jean-Sébastien and I ran up the stairs and past the sleeping guard. I glanced at my watch. No way would we make it back to town before curfew. It didn't matter. All that mattered was getting help. We had to get all those kids out of here — get Gaëlle away from Marie, and make sure Beatrice never set foot in this house again.

We ran up to the next landing. This was where I had first discovered last Friday that there was a basement and a glass door that had led me into the gardens. That seemed like a year ago, not a week.

I tapped Jean-Sébastien on the shoulder and pointed to the door we had just exited, urging him to remember exactly where it was. I didn't want to make a sound and risk waking the guard or alerting any servants who might be near. I understood why I had initially missed seeing it. It had some sort of coating that made it blend into the walls. Unless the moon shone directly on it through the small window opposite, like it did when I'd first seen it, and like it was doing now, that door was invisible.

Once we got out of the house, the full effect of what was going on hit me. Rage roiled inside me, and I felt the dream stone turn hot again.

How dare they!?

How dare they kidnap innocent children and torture them? How dare they hold children hostage in a prison I was sure was worse than any set up for hardened criminals? And how *dare* they plan to do this to sweet little Beatrice, who only wanted a mom and dad to love and call her own? The fury bubbled and boiled inside me. I could feel it increase with each realization of what they'd done to Mei, Gaëlle, and Olivia; to the others locked up in that horrid dungeon. And to all the girls they'd already sent away.

Why hasn't anyone — not so much as one single soul — ever questioned why every girl who gets adopted by these monsters withers instead of thrives? Why hasn't anyone asked why all the girls disappear and never return? Why hasn't anyone besides me thought something was very, very wrong at Irvigne Manor? The thoughts, the anger, and the shock all coursed through me at once, flooding me with emotion.

Or maybe those who had suspected things were wrong here hadn't lived to tell about it?

As I stood there wondering how people could treat other human beings so horribly, my fists clenched and unclenched at my sides. It felt like I had hot lava inside me. Lava that was rising to the top of a volcano getting ready to blow.

Just then, fierce barking echoed through the garden. Gaëlle had once mentioned that André and Marie kept dogs on the property for protection, but I hadn't seen any when I was there for the party. I sure could see them now, however. They were running toward us at full speed.

I watched in stunned horror as two enormous Rottweiler dogs barreled toward us across the lawn, their lips stretched back and their bared teeth gleaming.

"*Come on!*" Jean-Sébastien cried out. He grabbed my hand and pulled me toward the tree line. The dogs swerved and headed straight for us. They were just fifty meters away and closing in fast. There was no way we could make it to safety before they pounced and ripped us to shreds. I thought about trying to freeze the time again, but wouldn't that also freeze Jean-Sébastien in place?

I didn't even think twice about what I was doing — I just did it. I whipped around, full of fury, and planted my feet on the ground.

The magic swelled inside me like a tsunami about to break through a dam. Holding onto my dream stone, I drew a deep breath.

Roaring with all the ferocity of the angry Mama Bear, the pent-up stream of energy burst from within and slammed full-force into the Rottweilers.

It could only be magic — my witch magic.

One dog dropped to the ground with a whimper. The other somersaulted head over tail and landed in a heap beside his mate.

"*Go!*" I bellowed. "*Leave us alone!*" My voice, deep and thunderous, echoed in the silence of the night.

An ache throbbed in my chest as if the huge explosion of magic had blown a hole right through me. The dogs tucked their tails between their legs and ran away, yipping like a couple of coyote puppies.

I was glad I hadn't hurt the dogs and only scared them. It terrified me to think I could have hurt, or worse, *killed* a living creature.

"Ohhh-*kayyy*," Jean-Sébastien said, watching me with a wary expression. "Let this be a good reminder to *never* make you mad."

Great. Now Jean-Sébastien thinks I'm a freak, and by tomorrow, everyone in the orphanage and the Collège will know I'm a witch.

But to my surprise, Jean-Sébastien laughed. "That was the *coolest* thing I've ever watched anyone do. You are just full of surprises, Anna Sophia." He blew out a breath of relief. "I think that just took ten years off my life. Which is fine. If it weren't for you, those puppies would have *ended* my life. Man, I thought we were goners for sure."

I nodded, not trusting myself to say anything. I had thought we were goners, too.

"Remember when I said you were one strange girl?" He gave another nervous laugh. "Let me just amend that to say — you are, like… strange on steroids!" A low whistle escaped his lips as he shook his head in disbelief. "Good thing I'm not scared of strange, Anna Sophia." And then, looking right at me, he smiled.

Strange on steroids.

Yep, I thought. *I'd say that pretty well covers it.*

I shook the entire way back to the orphanage. Partially, it was from having used magic in front of Jean-Sébastien. But mostly, it was from the shock of what we had encountered in the basement. All I could think about was how much danger our friends were in, and how we had to find someone to help them right away.

As soon as Jean-Sébastien reached the orphanage door, I jumped off his motorbike and tossed him the helmet. "Go check on Beatrice," I shouted, running to the door. "She was with Marie and Gaëlle tonight!"

"But—"

"I'll find you later, Jean-Sébastien. I have to get help for them."

I saw him nod as I dashed inside.

Sisters Constance and Daphne were waiting for me. I knew they would be; it was way past curfew. They sat drinking tea in the small parlor to the left of the door. Before they could say a word, I raced into the parlor and burst into tears. Dropping to the floor in front of Sister Constance, I wrapped my arms around her legs and sobbed.

"Good heavens, Anna Sophia," Sister Daphne said in alarm. "What on earth happened?"

"Honestly, Daphne," Sister Constance said. "She's just trying to get out of trouble for violating curfew." But she didn't push me away, and her tone wasn't sharp at all. She almost sounded sort of… gentle.

"I—I know I'm in trouble," I said, my breath catching on every word. "Th—that… that's not why I'm crying!" I was sobbing so hard I could barely breathe. The second I saw them, the full horror of the night hit me. "You ha—hhhave to he—hhhelp them."

Sister Daphne left her chair and knelt next to me on the floor. "Anna… please try to calm down so you can tell us what is going on. What has happened? Has someone hurt you?"

"Nnnn—no, not me. The girls. Oh, it's so horrible. Please, *please*, you have to help them!"

The more I spoke, the more hysterical I became, as if saying the words out loud made everything so much more real.

"Anna, listen to me," Sister Daphne spoke gently but firmly as she put her hand on my back. "Whoever is in trouble can't be helped if you can't tell us what you are talking about. Take some deep breaths, Anna. We're right here."

She was right. Nobody could help Mei and the girls if I wasn't calm enough to tell the Sisters what I saw. I closed my eyes and breathed in deeply several times.

Sister Daphne handed me her handkerchief, and I blew my nose.

"I… I know leaving without telling you was wrong and I'm in big trouble, but please, please you must punish me later, because they need your help now. *Please*."

"Dear child!" Sister Constance exploded, her voice filled with exasperation. "If you cannot get out a complete sentence about what is going on, we cannot help anyone!"

"Constance," Sister Daphne said.

"Stop coddling the girl, Daphne. If someone's in trouble, we need to know who."

I nodded and blew my nose again. Taking a deep breath, I said, "Something bad has been happening at Irvigne Manor. I suspected it before, but last Friday at the party I saw even more things that made me suspicious. I made Jean-Sébastien take me there today because I knew André and Marie would be gone. I didn't say anything to you because I didn't think you'd believe me unless I had proof. We went to see if I could find out something specific."

"You and Jean-Sébastien went all the way out there on his motorbike?" Sister Constance interrupted. "What on—"

"Constance!" Sister Daphne interrupted. "Let's just allow Anna to finish the story. Please."

I nodded, surprised. I'd never heard Sister Daphne raise her voice before.

"Okay… so," I said, "when we got there, André and Marie were gone, and we went inside to check on Mei."

Sister Constance's eyebrows shot up as a look of disapproval crossed her face, but she didn't say anything about me just walking into that house.

"Go on, Anna. Did you find Mei?" Sister Daphne was obviously anxious, but her voice was gentle and encouraging. That helped me spit out the next part of what happened.

"I did." I burst into tears again. "She was locked up in a prison!"

Both Sisters gasped.

"N—not just Mei," I sputtered. "A… a bunch of kids."

I told them about the prison room with the terrible stench and the frightening torture chair in the middle. I repeated what Mei told me about how the older girls disappeared and were never heard from again. I described the look of sheer despair on Mei's face when she told me how André and Marie were going to adopt Beatrice and keep her, but send Mei, Gaëlle, and the other girls away. Just as soon as they had a ninth girl.

What I didn't tell them was that I was the ninth girl.

Sisters Briault both looked at me in horror as I gave them more and more details about what I'd seen. Sister Constance's mouth became thinner and thinner until finally she grabbed her cane and stomped it fiercely into the ground. Getting up, she wrapped her black knitted shawl around her shoulders and grabbed her purse. Her face was set in stony anger.

"Daphne, go check on Beatrice. Anna Sophia and I are going to talk to the police."

Sister Daphne gave my shoulder a squeeze and nodded at Sister Constance. When she stood up to leave the room, her face was so pale it looked drained of blood.

"Well, let's *go,* Anna!" Sister Constance demanded.

I jumped up and headed toward the door, feeling incredible relief that they believed me. I was also so glad Sister Daphne had gone to check on Beatrice, because, of course, Jean-Sébastien couldn't have checked on her: He wasn't allowed on the girl's side of the orphanage.

Chapter 26

ear Diary,

I'm so relieved Sister Constance believed me and is taking me to the police station. I've never been to one before, and I feel scared, which seems so silly. Why should I be afraid of the people who could save my friends? I'm sure I'll just need to give them a statement, and then they'll go right over to Irvigne Manor and arrest those terrible people. It's not like it's going to be difficult to find proof I'm telling them the truth — that's for sure.

It seems odd to feel so much anxiety when, in just a few minutes, the police will go there to free all the girls from that awful place. I must be overwrought from this whole experience because I should be feeling relief, not concern.

Actually, I just remembered another thing Sister Agnes had read us from Malala Yousafzai's book. In her book, Malala asks the question: "If one man can destroy everything, why can't one girl change it?"

It's such a good question, and recalling it gives me more confidence. Because it's true for me as well, right? If those dreadful people can destroy the lives of so many girls, well, then why can't I do what I need to do to give them their lives back?

I can!

And I'm leaving right now with Sister Constance to do just that!

I'll write more later, Diary. I'll write after we've been to the police station and I know all the girls are safe. That will be a much happier letter to you.

Over the years, Sister Constance had often scared or intimidated me with her stern demeanor. She was so serious and rule-driven, I used to wonder if she even knew *how* to smile. But as we walked the three blocks to the local police station, I was sure there wasn't anyone I would have rather had with me. Her determination to get help for all those girls trapped in Irvigne Manor's prison reminded me of Mama Bear when she was protecting her cubs from danger.

She was that fierce!

The lights of the police station were so bright we spotted them from a full block away. For some reason, I found this oddly comforting. Maybe I thought something so bright and visible could only be good, it was difficult to say. What I did know was the feeling disappeared the second we pressed the security doorbell.

That was when a gruff, unpleasant voice barked, "State your business." He didn't say "hello," or "can I help you," or anything.

Sister Constance didn't seem the least bit bothered by his rudeness. Without hesitating, she barked right back. "We are here to report a kidnapping," she said, and she thumped her cane into the pavement twice to emphasize the importance of our being there.

I expected a flurry of activity to happen when they heard why we were there. I thought maybe a whole crew of constables would race to the door to let us in. But, in fact, nothing happened.

Nothing.

After what seemed like an hour, but was probably only a couple of minutes, I assumed we weren't going to be allowed inside. I glanced at Sister Constance, who grimaced and pressed her lips into a thin, angry line. She was just getting ready to press the buzzer again when we heard a loud clicking sound.

The same unpleasant voice said, "Close the door firmly behind you."

Sister Constance sniffed and muttered something about people not having manners anymore. Her back erect, she walked stiffly into the building. I followed and made sure the door closed tightly behind us. Whoever that voice belonged to was not someone I cared to make angry. At least, not before I told him about Irvigne Manor.

The station turned out to be small, and only one constable appeared to be on duty. It seemed safe to assume it was his voice that we had heard from outside. My first thought was that he certainly looked as unpleasant as he sounded. He was tall, with a massive belly that made me wonder how he could ever capture a bad guy when, surely, he couldn't run five meters without collapsing. And his skin had a greenish gray color that looked like it had never seen the sun. A name tag on his shirt read, "Ouellette."

"Constable… *Ouellette,* is it?" Sister Constance said, staring at him. When he didn't respond, she added, "Are you listening, young man? We are here to report a possible kidnapping!"

"A *definite* kidnapping," I said. I started to say more, but Sister Constance held up her hand to silence me.

"This young lady is in my charge at the Collège du Parc Cézanne, and she has been witness to several children who are being held against their will." Sister Constance pursed her lips together making it look like she had just sucked on a lemon. She tapped her cane against the floor while she waited for his response.

"And where did this alleged kidnapping take place?" Constable Ouellette asked, sounding bored and looking irritated.

"At Irvigne Manor," I said before Sister Constance could stop me. I was about to tell him I expected constables to be helpful, but thought better of it and said nothing else.

His eyebrows snaked together. He looked at me, then at Sister Constance, and then back at me. His eyes bored into mine for what felt like several long minutes.

"Come with me," he snapped. We followed him down a short corridor to a room with a small wall plaque on the outside of the door that said, "Interrogation."

"You sit in there," he said, pointing me toward the room. "You wait out here." He looked at Sister Constance and pointed to a chair along the wall.

"I'll do no such thing!" Sister Constance said as she puffed up her chest and stood tall. She barely reached the constable's nose, but when she waved her cane in his face, he backed off a step. "I already told you this young lady is in my charge. And she will remain so. If you wish to take her statement, you will do so in my presence. Is that understood, young man?"

Constable Ouellette mumbled an apology. I wasn't surprised Sister Constance could make this bully of a constable feel like a naughty schoolboy. She had the gift.

A bare bulb hanging from the ceiling provided the only light in the interrogation room. It cast odd shadows on the walls and did the man's ghastly green color no favors. The room had only one small table and two chairs, so Constable Ouellette brought in the chair from the corridor. He placed two chairs for Sister Constance and me on one side of the table, while he sat to face us from the other. To my surprise, Sister Constance chose to stand.

He picked up a small notebook and pen from the table and said, "Start from the beginning and make sure to state specific details."

I started by telling him about Mei and how she didn't go to school anywhere. Then I told him about the party on Friday and how I'd overheard André and the Black Horseman talking about captives.

"I was worried because Mei looked so scared and stressed," I said. "So I went to the house today to look for her."

He tapped the pen against his chin.

"And the Montmorencys let you into their home? To look for your friend?"

"Well, they weren't actually home," I said, trying not to squirm. "The door was open, so I just walked in."

Well, okay, that was a lie. I just hoped it was a forgivable one because I couldn't very well say I walked through an iron door to get inside.

"While inside," I continued, "I found Mei in the basement with six other kids. They're still there, locked up in horrible, filthy cells! And you ha—"

Constable Ouellette held up a hand. "Wait a minute. You expect me to believe that André and Marie Montmorency, two of our most upstanding citizens, have children locked up in their basement?"

"Yes! I know it sounds crazy, but it's true. I heard the guy with the ponytail — the one they call the Black Horseman — say there had to be nine children. Mei and Olivia and Gaëlle, along with the five others I saw locked up but don't know, add up to eight. They're going to adopt Beatrice and keep her around for show, but send those eight and a ninth girl away!"

Constable Ouellette glared at me like I was the one who kidnapped them.

"And I think I'm the one they're waiting for — the ninth girl," I blurted out, hoping that would shock him into realizing I was telling the truth.

To my surprise, Sister Constance took my hand and squeezed it. At least I knew she believed me. The police would too, as soon as they went to Irvigne Manor and rescued those girls.

Finally, I saw Constable Ouellette write something in his notebook. He hadn't taken any notes the whole time I had been telling him everything I saw happening over there. I thought that was strange.

I was just about to shout at him and tell him we were wasting time. I wanted to tell him he needed to get over there right now. But before I could say a word, he sat back in his chair and tipped it on two legs. He glared at me with this angry intensity that shocked me. As he continued to bore his eyes into mine, I found myself unable to speak. It became hard to breathe. I couldn't move my eyes away from his, and I watched as they turned solid black. He continued to stare at me, and suddenly I understood: There was *magic* in his glare.

My bones started to turn soft, and I knew if I tried to stand or run, my body would collapse.

His magic coiled around me in a circle. Every second, it got tighter and tighter as it pushed all the available air outside of this circle. I began to suffocate, and my hands rose to my throat. *I can't breathe!* I screamed inside my head. *I can't breathe!*

I felt like I was inside one of those plastic travel bags people use to compress their clothes. The kind where all the air gets sucked out and the bag is sealed shut.

I saw a small smile tug at the corner of Constable Ouellette's mouth just as the room started to get fuzzy and turn black.

He's going to kill me! I thought, starting to lose mental focus. *Right here, right now, he's going to kill me if I don't do something. But… what can I do?*

As clearly as if he were standing next to me, I heard Uncle Misha's voice. "*Believe in yourself,* Malyshka. *Trust that you possess more bravery than fear. He may be tough, but you are tougher.*"

I have more bravery than fear? That was hard to believe considering how terrified I felt at that moment. However, with my fading consciousness I managed to think, *Uncle Misha is right… I came to help those girls, and I won't let Ouellette stop me.*

Using all the little strength left in me, I willed my magic to come together and form a stiff, powerful ball in my stomach. It felt warm, then hot, and it grew hotter still as it expanded through my body and limbs and pushed back against Ouellette's. Right before it blew out of me like lava from a volcano, it turned a brilliant red and aimed itself at the constable.

The stream of my magic slammed into his chest. In some sort of silent awe, I watched as his chair blew backward and he crashed to the floor.

The notebook he had been holding fell onto the table and landed face up. I managed to read his underlined note:

She's the one!

She's the one!

Chapter 27

Constable Ouellette brushed himself off as he apprehensively glanced in my direction. I doubted he had expected me to fight back. It was unlikely he even knew I had the power to do that. I felt a little stunned myself by what I had done. But what shocked me even more was the realization that Constable Ouellette possessed the ability to use magic. I had never thought about other people in my town having magical powers.

Is he a man-witch, a warlock? I thought. *How is that possible?* I glanced at Sister Constance, who had moved away from the wall and was strutting toward him.

"That will teach you to keep four on the floor, young man!" she said, pointing her cane and waving it in front of him. "I should think you would know this at your age."

Didn't she see what happened? Did Sister Constance think his chair just... tipped over?

I wondered if maybe I had imagined the fiery red stream of energy speeding out of my chest and hitting Ouellette. I didn't *think* I had, but then why hadn't Sister Constance noticed? She had been standing right behind me.

Constable Ouellette mumbled another one of his lame apologies to Sister Constance and told us we were free to leave.

I looked at Sister Constance in surprise. She nodded curtly toward the constable, and asked, "What about the girls?" She tapped her cane impatiently as she stared directly at him.

"I will check on Irvigne Manor myself." He made it a point not to look my way. "And I will inform you if I find anything there."

"I will wait to hear from you, then," Sister Constance said. "I expect you to bring those girls home, young man. Promptly." She turned to me. "Come, Anna. Let's leave, and let the good constable do his job."

Good constable? I didn't know what to think. It had been one of the scariest nights of my life, but Sister Constance didn't seem to think anything strange had happened. Now we were going back to the orphanage, and I had no idea what Ouellette would do. He had, after all, tried to kill me. I could only hope he would hurry over to Irvigne Manor and rescue Mei and Gaëlle, and the others.

But would he? I honestly doubted that, but I didn't know what to do. Should I go to another police station, run to the Manor, or should I just run away?

I was getting totally confused. Maybe I had imagined Constable Ouelette's attempt to kill me, and what I had experienced there was some sort of nervous reaction to all the stress of the last few days. He was a policeman; and if I couldn't trust the Swiss Police, then *who* could I trust? Maybe I had lashed out at him for nothing.

As we walked home, Sister Constance surprised me by saying, "I realize you think I am overly critical of people, and just an old Fuddy Duddy, Anna Sophia. But that was a very strange man back there. I believe even my Pollyanna sister, Daphne would have found him not quite right in the head." She thumped her cane and grumbled. "Didn't care for him, I must say. Poor excuse for a man of the law."

I wanted to stop right there in the street and hug her. I even wanted to pour out the whole story about my magic because, when he was suffocating me, it was the most helpless feeling I'd ever had in my life. If Uncle Misha hadn't popped into my head, I would be dead... And nobody would have ever even known a policeman had murdered me.

Thinking about Uncle Misha made me wonder about being able to hear his voice. How was he able to speak to me so clearly? I assumed it was just my desperate imagination, and I decided to think about it later. What I needed to understand immediately was what Sister Constance thought happened in the station.

"In what way did you find him strange?" I asked. I wanted to push her a little and see if she sensed any of his magic.

"*In what way?* Well, my goodness! For starters, he had fewer manners than a street urchin. And he doesn't seem to brush his teeth nearly often enough. Good heavens, his breath stank of garlic. Honestly, you'd think a man who deals with the public all day would use mints once in a while."

That made me giggle, but it also made me realize she was only bothered by obvious things. I decided not to say anything about the magic — neither his, nor mine.

Sister Daphne stood waiting for us in the Collège entrance hall.

"Beatrice is home safe," she said. "She's all excited about going to live in the castle with the Montmorencys though..."

I could see she'd been crying by her red-rimmed eyes. Poor Sister Daphne. She loved every single one of us so much. And after tonight, I saw that Sister Constance did, too. She just showed it differently.

"Well, after today, the Montmorencys won't be able to hurt Beatrice or any other child," Sister Constance said. "The constable assured us he would look into the matter immediately. Now you, young lady, off to bed."

I thanked her for taking me to the police station, and on a whim, I kissed her wrinkled face. She muttered something about cheeky girls and shooed me up the stairs.

I thought I'd never fall asleep. Visions of Mei's tear-stained face kept popping into my mind, and I couldn't stop worrying about Beatrice. We would save her from a terrible fate, but she was going to be heartbroken once she learned she couldn't live in a castle and be part of a real family.

When I finally fell asleep, I had terrible nightmares of the Black Horseman chasing me through a forest of hedges. His deep voice echoed through the trees: *She's the one! She's the one!*

I woke in a sweat. Not knowing exactly why, I got up and took Squire out of my backpack. Once I was back in bed, I found myself hugging him to my chest like a teddy bear.

I woke again, this time to the sound of someone pounding on my door.

Stumbling out of bed, I threw on my bathrobe and slippers and opened the door to find two constables standing there, their faces stern and aloof. I recognized one of them as Constable Ouellette.

"Anna Sophia, you are under arrest for the murder of Mei Montmorency," he said.

"What?" My mind refused to register what they were saying. "Mei isn't dead. I just saw her last night. You were supposed to rescue her. You said you would!"

"Mei Montmorency has been missing for a week," Constable Ouellette said. "Your story was a complete fabrication, made up to cover up your horrendous crime."

I realized I was still gripping Squire in one hand. Remembering the nightmares that had caused me to get up and find him, I felt dread rising in my chest. I dropped Squire into the pocket of my robe just before the other constable grabbed my shoulder painfully, and clamped handcuffs over my wrists.

"I didn't hurt anybody!" I yelled. "You *know* that. You know I told you the truth!"

The constable jerked me into the hallway. A group of girls, still wearing pajamas, had gathered by the stairs. Lauraleigh pushed through them.

"Where are you taking Anna?" she demanded. Her messy hair fell across her eyes, and she pushed it away impatiently.

"This girl is the prime suspect in a murder case," said the constable, whose name tag read "Barnabé."

My legs felt like they were about to buckle from fear, and my stomach flip-flopped with every breath. I tried to speak but couldn't get a single word through the lump in my throat.

Lauraleigh stepped in front of us before the constables could drag me down the stairs. "You can't just take her away like this!" she cried out.

They shoved her out of the way and descended the stairs, pushing me in front of them. As they poked me in the back, I kept stumbling.

They had managed to ignore Lauraleigh. But, at the bottom of the stairs was a force not easy to ignore, and it stopped both constables in their tracks.

"What is the meaning of this?" Sister Constance said icily. "And, I daresay, how did you get in here without my knowledge? The front door is always locked after ten p.m.!"

She wore a gray bathrobe and an old-fashioned hairnet over a head full of curlers. She had her cane raised in front of her like a weapon. "I'm *waiting*, Constable Ouellette!"

The constables glanced at each other uncomfortably. It was obvious they had picked the lock to get inside.

Ouellette pulled himself to his full height and stuck his chin out defiantly. "This girl is wanted for the murder of Mei Montmorency."

"That's ridiculous," Sister Constance said with a dismissive chortle. "What proof do you have?"

The constable waved a piece of paper in front of her face. "This warrant for her arrest is all the proof I need. Now move out of my way, or I'll arrest you for obstruction of justice."

Sister Constance glared at the two constables. Her eyes darkened with fury, and her lips paled from being stretched into a hard, thin line. She grabbed the paper and read it.

After a moment, my heart sank as she moved aside. Constable Barnabé jabbed me between my shoulders and pushed me forward.

"Don't you worry, child," Sister Constance said. "I'll call Monsieur Nolan, and he'll take care of this *immediately*."

Please, please don't let them take me away, I wanted to cry out and beg. I desperately wanted to throw my arms around Sister Constance's legs so they couldn't move me. But my hands were bound behind me, and constable Barnabé shoved me forward before I could utter a single word.

"Freeze," I whispered under my breath. "Freeze!"

But nothing and no one froze around me. I wondered if Ouellette was somehow blocking my magical abilities, or if I was too distraught to use them.

Another crowd of onlookers had gathered outside, drawn by the flashing lights and noise. Tears blurred my vision as I was shoved into the back of a police cruiser.

"Get in there and don't make a fuss," Barnabé grumbled. Ouellette started the car and turned on the siren.

There's no reason for the siren, I thought. *They just want to attract as much attention as possible, so everyone thinks I'm a murderer.*

Finally, I felt rage blossoming in my chest. I knew I could release it like I had done with the Rottweilers. Ouellette and Barnabé would never know what hit them.

It would feel so good. They would deserve anything I sent their way.

But it wouldn't solve the problem, I realized. I'd still be a murder suspect.

I needed to wait. I had to figure out how I could use my magic in the best, most useful way. Plus, I needed to give Monsieur Nolan a chance to fix everything. He was a well-known and respected solicitor, and he knew lots of important people in high-up positions. I knew he would go to the ends of the earth for me, and I needed to give him the chance to save me and all the girls at Irvigne Manor.

I was worried, though, because now I knew Ouellette was more than just a constable. He knew magic, and I had no idea what things he could do or control with it. I needed to watch him closely and learn as much about him as I could.

I had been so deep in thought I hadn't noticed the siren was off. I did, however, notice we had driven right past the police station and were heading out of town. "Where are you taking me?" I asked. Neither of them answered, but Barnabé looked back at me and smirked.

This was bad. Monsieur Nolan would be heading for the police station by the orphanage. If they were taking me somewhere else, how would he find me?

Fifteen minutes later, we turned up the twisting mountain road. They were taking me to Irvigne Manor!

"You're not even real constables, are you?" I asked through clenched teeth.

"I am," Ouellette responded in a light tone. "Been on the force for over ten years. Barnabé here has been in uniform for just a few hours, but it looks good on him, don't you think?"

My mind whirled, trying to fit the pieces of the puzzle together. Ouellette must be telling the truth because he'd been at the station last night. So, it was just Barnabé who was a hired criminal. But why? Why were they doing this?

Then it hit me. Maybe Barnabé wasn't the only hired crook.

Without even thinking it through, I blurted out, "You work for the Black Horseman, don't you?"

The realization of this stunned me. And scared me. I didn't know what made me say it, but as soon as it was out of my mouth, I felt the truth of it.

"You'd do well to keep your mouth shut," Ouellette said with a sneer. He pressed the gas pedal, causing us to zoom up the twisting road at a frightening speed. No one had bothered to buckle me in, and every turn in the road sent me banging against one side door or the other. I thought about jumping out, but the police car was made to hold captives and there were no handles on the rear doors. I couldn't have done it anyway, because my hands were still cuffed behind my back.

I need to use my magic. But how? How could I hit Ouellette with enough force to knock him out, yet not kill myself in the process?

I didn't have a clue. I just knew there wasn't any other choice but to try.

I pictured all my magic coiled into a tight ball in my stomach, like a serpent getting ready to strike… But before I could do anything more, Ouellette slammed on the brakes. I hit the front seat hard enough to bruise my shoulder and lose control of the magic.

Bam! Just that fast, it was gone.

Barnabé opened the rear door and dragged me out of the car. The road was bumpy and uneven. Rocks poked through my thin slippers, bruising my feet. It was dark, and I couldn't tell exactly where we were, but we had to be close to the top of the mountain. The headlights were directed to the edge of the cliff where everything dropped off into a tumble of rocks and bracken, all the way down to the river.

It would be a deadly fall.

Ouellette grabbed my shoulder and jerked me away from the car. "Stand here and don't make any trouble." He turned to Barnabé. "He'll be here any minute. Get it done."

Barnabé nodded. He took two huge bricks out of the trunk. The front of the car was already pointing toward the cliff. I watched as he dropped the bricks on the gas pedal, causing the engine to roar. Horrified, I saw him grab the shift lever and put the car into drive.

The car bucked once before racing forward. One terrifying moment later, I watched it soar over the embankment. Fender over fender, it flew, before dropping out of sight. Then glass shattered. Metal screeched and broke apart. There was a strange whining sound right before it hit the bottom of the ravine and exploded into towering flames.

"Isn't that pretty. Nothing like a good bonfire," Ouellette said with a grin. He turned to me. "Pity, isn't it? No one could survive a crash like that." He laughed. "And now, all your friends will think you're dead."

I stared at him, half in shock and half in absolute rage.

"No one will care," he said, ignoring my expression. "Why would they? You'll just be another dead orphan nobody cares about. Well, except to be relieved, perhaps, since *this* dead orphan had murdered her friend." He smiled. "Good riddance to you, eh, Anna Sophia?"

He made a disgusting sound by clicking his tongue twice on the roof of his mouth. *Click, click.* It made me want to vomit.

A car came flying down the road. It screeched to a halt within inches of us, sending dirt and rocks flying everywhere.

André stepped out of the passenger's side. Even that early in the morning, he was wearing an impeccable white suit with a royal blue handkerchief poking out of the jacket pocket.

“Hello, Number Nine,” he said, his voice booming. “Welcome home.”

PART III: Courage

Courage:
The ability to do things that scare you;
bravery or valor.

Chapter 28

André shoved me into the back seat of the car, chuckling to himself. He got into the front passenger seat. He turned around to glare at me, and I couldn't believe just how evil he looked. I never liked André, but I never thought of him to be that demonic. For all I knew, he might even *be* the Devil. Who else would do this — abduct young girls for who knew what fate?

"You thought you were so clever, didn't you, little witch," he said, looking at me with disgust in his eyes. "Well now, you're about to find out just how clever you are *not*." His tone sent chills up and down my neck.

Ouellette and Barnabé got in the back of the car, sandwiching me between them. Even if my hands hadn't been handcuffed, I wouldn't have been able to move.

I had no idea who the driver was, and I had a feeling nobody was going to tell me. Without being able to lean forward, I couldn't even get a good look at him to see if it was someone I knew. I wanted to know if it was the Black Horseman. Eventually, I noticed he had a mask over his head, so I might not be able to tell even if I did manage to get a look at him.

Or *her*. It wouldn't have surprised me one bit to discover it was Marie driving the car.

I still couldn't believe this was all happening. I was so mad I wanted to spit and kick, and rip André's eyes out. Inside me, my magic was bubbling and churning in all sorts of ways, but I was so angry I couldn't focus to do anything with it. I felt it building and growing, and getting hotter and hotter.

André tossed a fat envelope to each constable. "Once we arrive at Irvigne Manor, you two will disappear. This cash will cover your fees and travel expenses." He turned back to face the road and said nothing else.

Barnabé opened his envelope and counted the money. He nodded with a satisfied grunt.

Ouellette tucked his envelope into a shirt pocket without looking at it. "I think I should stay until the boss arrives," he said.

The boss? If the Black Horseman is his boss, then I guess he isn't driving. More and more I suspected it was Marie driving the car. I thought it was kind of funny that if it was true, she was too chicken to show her face.

Figures.

"I want to keep an eye on this one," Ouellette stated, jabbing me in the arm with his fat finger.

"Oh, you think I can't guard the little girl?" André asked over his shoulder. There was a dangerous edge to his voice.

"Not saying that," Ouellette responded casually. "Just pays to be cautious."

Ouellette didn't seem at all intimidated by André, and I guessed it was because André wasn't his boss. If I was right, that person would be the nameless man with the ponytail — the Black Horseman.

André glared at Ouellette in the rear-view mirror and grunted. "Perhaps you're right," he said. "Caution is always called for when dealing with witches." He grinned at me. "Yes, little witch, we know all about you. Are you surprised, Anna Sophia? Thanks to our friend, we probably know more about your exalted family than you do."

Our friend?

If things grew any hotter inside me, I might've just blown all of us up. I needed to ignore André and focus on controlling my growing magic.

I took a deep breath and forced myself to casually look away. *Breathe into your magic*, I told myself. *Control it.*

André continued to leer at me. "But don't worry. We know exactly how to take care of witches at Irvigne Manor."

Oh, you think so, do you? Well, maybe you should think again, André.

I felt the coiled serpent return and ready to strike. It was nesting inside me on a bed of red-hot fury churning and bubbling all around it. André was half-turned toward me, and I could see his lips moving but I couldn't hear his words. All my senses were focused on the cobra of energy waiting for me set it free. I wanted to unleash every inch of the hot anger that had created the coiled beast.

But I didn't.

Once again, Uncle Misha's voice came to guide me. It was just like in the police station — as vivid and real as if he had been standing beside me. "Malyshka, *remember*," the voice said. "*You must always be kinder than necessary. Every act of kindness grows your spirit and strengthens your soul. Don't forget this, Anna Sophia, my sweet* Malyshka."

My sweet *Malyshka*. Uncle Misha always called me this in the most loving way. I knew he wasn't scolding me, but rather he was reminding me of something I had already learned from him. Because Uncle Misha was the wisest person I'd ever known, his words made me stop and think. If kindness grew your spirit, what did meanness do? If it strengthened your soul, what would happen to mine if I used my magic to harm others?

I wanted to destroy André, I did. But I didn't want to use magic in a way that would end up turning me into someone like him.

So I spat a little of my energy out.

Oh, Sister Constance would have had a *coronary* if she'd seen me do that. Girls did *not* spit in her world. However, I couldn't think of any other way to release only a small amount of what was coiled up so tightly inside me.

My small blast of energy hit the handkerchief in André's pocket. It caught fire like it had been soaked in gasoline and I'd put a match to it. Instantly, flames whooshed into the air.

André screamed like the howler monkey we'd learned about in science class. His yelp was so loud I was sure they could hear it back at the orphanage. I wanted to cover my ears. Ouellette whimpered, complaining about the pain in his ears, and Barnabé tried to bury his head behind me. I didn't let him, of course. I leaned forward so he wouldn't get any protection from me.

André went from screaming to bellowing as he swatted his chest and cursed.

I couldn't help it. I smiled — if only a little bit.

It wasn't a big fire, and he put it out without getting injured or causing a major mess in the car. He was fine, but his gazillion-dollar suit was ruined, which I found strangely satisfying.

That's just a taste of what I can do, I thought as I fell back against the seat. *I'll find a way to free those girls — just you wait and see.*

The only problem was, I didn't know exactly how I was going to do it. What I did know was that, somehow, I'd figure it out.

When we arrived at Irvigne Manor, I expected André to take me to the dungeon and put me in one of those cells near Mei. But he didn't. Instead, he had Ouellette march me into one of the towers and up a spiral staircase. A single room occupied the top floor. Just before he shoved me into it, Ouellette *finally* unlocked my handcuffs.

"You shouldn't have done that to André." He glared at me. "If you weren't good as dead before, you sure are now." He laughed as he slammed the door shut. He probably wanted to pretend I hadn't seen him snivel like the baby he was, but we both knew I had. And we both knew he was weaker than me. All he had that I didn't was the key to my prison.

"Bye-bye, stupid little witch," he sneered from the other side of the door. I heard the click of a key locking it.

I rubbed my bruised wrists as I looked around the room. It wasn't much better than the dungeon cells. It was dim, lit only by one light bulb. It had bare stone floors, bare walls, and a dirty mattress shoved into one corner. Broken furniture, crumpled papers, and piles of books littered the rest of the room. It looked like it had once been someone's library, or maybe an office.

The room had one big window. By this time it was morning, and streaks of light leaked through cracks in the shutters. I opened them, pressed my head against the glass and peered out. It was a very long drop to the ground. Way too far for me to jump, for sure.

The only good thing at all was that I could see my faithful moon in the brightening sky. Knowing she was there made me feel less alone.

Initially, I wished they had put me with Mei and the other girls, so we could have talked to each other and come up with an escape plan. I probably would've had to tell them I was a witch however, and that might not have gone over so well. So, maybe it *was* better they put me in the tower. Except, escape was going to be harder than it would have been from the dungeon.

Which André, no doubt, knew.

I could probably walk right through the door, I thought, turning away from the window to look at it. *It's just a flimsy wooden one.*

I stood there, staring at the door. *If I walked through brick and iron, surely, I can walk through a little bit of wood.*

And right into Constable Ouellette, who was likely standing guard at the bottom of the steps, waiting for the Black Horseman.

Clearly, walking through the door or walls wasn't going to work in the tower.

I had to find a way out of there. If I didn't, they would send Gaëlle, Mei, Olivia, and all those others away. I couldn't jump out the window. I couldn't walk through the door. And I sure as heck couldn't fly out the window.

Or… could I?

Chapter 29

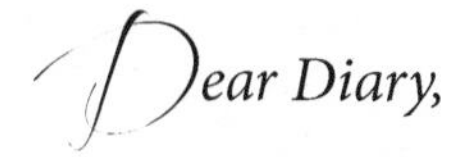*ear Diary,*

I'm writing to you in my head. I have no pen, and I'm stuck in a room in the tower, just like Rapunzel. Well, except I don't have long golden hair to hang down so someone can climb up and rescue me.

So much for writing you after the girls were rescued. It hasn't happened, at least not yet. I thought I'd go to the police and everything would be fine. Instead, now I'm locked up just like everybody else.

I wish I knew how to fly, like that old witch in the picture that my mother had sent me. If I did, I could just open the window and soar away. And then I would find an honest constable to come and help get all the girls away from here. One who would send André, Marie, Ouellette, and the Black Horseman straight to prison.

Forever.

But I can't fly, even though I think it is something witches do... Or maybe they only do that in fairy tales? I wish I knew.

I suppose the only thing to do is try. Right? It's not like I have a lot of other options available to me here.

Wish me luck, Diary!

I looked around the room, thinking maybe I could find a broom. Not that it looked like anyone had swept in there any time in the last century, but brooms were what witches used for flying. At least that's what they used in any picture I'd ever seen.

I didn't find a broom, only a mop in a bucket. A disgusting, moldy, smelly, tangled mess of a mop. *Still,* I thought, *a mop is kind of a broom*. Right? It also had a handle. It was at least worth giving it a try.

I felt ridiculous. I grimaced and sat on that mop's handle, like I was riding a hobbyhorse.

"Um… giddyup?" I said cautiously. Nothing. "Abracadabra?" Still nothing. I ran around the cluttered room, feeling like an idiot and getting nowhere.

I dumped it back in the bucket and looked at the mattress. It was crawling with bugs.

Gross.

I sat down on one of the rickety chairs. It was fine, other than needing a book under one of the legs.

There had to be some magic I could use to escape. Supposedly, I was from a whole family of witches. *Exalted* family of witches. Isn't that what André called them? There must be something in my bloodline to give me escape powers.

I was sure my mother would have told me all these things in her letter; she just didn't have enough time. It made me sad to think once again that she'd used her last breath to write me. Even more, it made me sad to think of all the things she could have taught me had she lived.

Well, getting depressed isn't going to help you get out of here, I told myself sharply. *You need a plan!*

I wished I could make André tell me about my family, so I might get a clue how to use my powers. Not that he would ever tell me such things — he wouldn't, of course. It was driving me crazy to think he knew things about them I didn't.

How does he know about my family, anyway?

Just thinking of André's smug face made my fists clench in rage. I should have burned more than just his handkerchief. I wished the flames had set his hair on fire. And eyebrows, too! That would have shown him what a girl from a family of *exalted witches* could do! I was working myself up into a frenzy of rage.

"Malyshka. *What are you thinking, child? Have you forgotten the greatest of all powers is the power to be kind?*" Uncle Misha's voice was whispering his words in my ear.

A little later, I heard a new voice — not Uncle Misha's, certainly. I didn't know who it was; I had never heard it before.

"Anna," the new voice said. The voice was female, and she pronounced my name like with an odd accent: *Ahh-na*. She sounded young like me.

"*Ahh-na... I'll tell you what my soul told me. My soul said, 'Be peaceful. Love everyone.' Do you understand, Ahh-na? You must not treat others with cruelty. You must fight some of them, yes; but through peace.*"

A third voice spoke softly in my other ear. *"Anna, Malala is correct. In the long run, the sharpest weapon of all is a kind and gentle spirit."*

I felt like my head was spinning, and the stress of my sudden captivity seemed to be turning me crazy. *Malala?*

That last voice I'd imagined must have belonged to Anne Frank, because I knew she wrote about the sharpest weapon. I read it in her book.

I looked around, just to make sure I was still alone in the room. Uncle Misha wasn't there. Certainly, neither Malala nor

Anne Frank were there. Yet, I had heard all three speak to me as clearly as if they were standing next to me, and I wondered if I had just experienced one of my new witchy powers, some sort of ability to tap into information floating around us in the world.

The other alternative — that I was beginning to break under stress and develop multiple personalities — disturbed me too much to think about.

I remembered something else Uncle Misha used to tell me. He said if a person loses the kindness of their spirit, a dark shadow will take its place in their heart.

Is that what I felt in the car? When I was so happy to see André's handkerchief on fire, was I killing the kindness in me and letting in the shadows?

I felt scared. Not just because I heard those voices, although, for sure, that was a little freaky. I was also scared because I started to suspect that my magic could be dangerous or bad. I started to wonder if maybe I was a *black* witch, like that old woman in my mother's picture.

Is that the kind of family I'm from — a family who used black magic?

I rubbed my chest, wishing I could send away the darkness I now believed lived inside me. I wished I had someone to help me, someone to answer all the questions I needed answered. Someone to assure me I wasn't born from darkness.

Then I remembered.

Squire!

He was still in my pocket. I pulled him out, but of course, he was lifeless and cold. I just needed some fire to bring him to life. I searched the drawers of the broken desk for a candle or matches — there were none. The room had no fireplace, and a quick glance at the piles of books told me I would find no help there.

Wait! I've made fire.

I had made fire to light up André's handkerchief. I could do it again and wake up Squire.

But would using my magic bring in more of that shadow? I didn't know.

I sat there, thinking about it for quite a long time. Finally, I decided it was a risk I had to take. I couldn't think of any other way to get answers, and maybe even get help in getting out of there. I just hoped if I used my magic for good, and not for creating harm, it would keep the shadow away.

I rolled a stack of papers into a torch and concentrated on locating the now-familiar magical energy inside of me. I didn't want to set the whole room on fire any more than I wanted to set the whole car on fire. I knew I could blow out just a little bit of magic if I focused on it, because that's what I'd done back in the car.

The problem was, it was so much harder to find the magic when I wasn't angry or desperately scared. Each time I'd experienced it, it was just there — like in the police station, or when I lit up André's handkerchief. Now that I wasn't feeling an immediate sense of rage toward someone, there wasn't a roiling, boiling mass of hot energy gathering inside me. Without it, I had no way to access my magic.

I had two choices. I could go inside myself and find the magic, or I could make myself angry enough for it to find me.

I closed my eyes and looked inside my own mind. I breathed deeply once, twice, and I kept breathing just as deeply until the room and the little noises surrounding me — the sound of wind outside, the tiny rattles of the window frames, the creaking of the old floor boards — faded away. After a long time of hard concentration, I found myself in such complete stillness that even my own body disappeared from my awareness, and only my mind remained.

And there it was: All my magic was there, waiting. It seemed to reside in the pit of my stomach. I could feel its energy, and I could even imagine reaching out and touching it. It felt warm and sparkly, and it glimmered with all kinds of colors I hadn't seen before: blue and turquoise, red and yellow, and there even were some orange and black hues. I conjured up a mental image of gathering a handful of sparkly red flames and rolling them into a small ball.

It was like two of me began to exist at the same time: one watching, and one doing. In that way, I watched myself as I held the ball of flames close to my lips and blew a smooth breath of fire toward the paper. And then, as if I had lit a candle, the paper became a gentle torch of small and quiet flames.

Smiling, I held Squire above it, hoping he would wake up before the papers burned out.

Chapter 30

Squire exploded into his animated self and rocketed around the room. I watched him, feeling relieved to see him awake.

"I'm so happy to see you," I said. "But we don't have any time to spare, Squire. We're in big trouble."

He immediately zoomed from the ceiling to float in front of me. As quickly as I could, I filled him in on what had happened. I started by telling him about the girls locked up in cells. I described how Constable Ouellette and the fake policeman had woken me up in the middle of the night and made it look like I had died in a car explosion. I finished by saying, "And, now, André has me imprisoned in this tower. The door is locked, and I'm sure someone is guarding it. Probably Ouellette."

Squire zipped over to the window and hovered for a moment. He returned, opened his fingers wide, and arched them back in an apparent expression of surprise.

"I know, right?" I sighed. "We are way, *way* high up. I tried to fly like a real witch, but it didn't work. There isn't even a broom in here. Only a mop. Truthfully, I don't even know if witches do fly on brooms. That might just be what's in folktales."

I paused and chewed on the inside of my lip. "And even if it's true, Squire, and even if there was a broom, I'm not sure I should ever use my magic again. I think it brings in the darkness."

Squire made a motion like writing.

"Of course!" I said. "Sorry I didn't think of it sooner. I think I lost my brain somewhere between finding the girls and getting locked up!"

I searched around the room for the paper and pen I knew Squire needed. Finding paper was easy; old books were littered everywhere, and many had blank pages in the back. Fortunately, after a bit of rummaging around, I also found an old pencil stub. I handed him both, and he quickly started writing.

"You are a real witch. And they do fly."

"How come it didn't work for me?"

"When you both want to and need to, you will find your way of flying."

Well, that was strange. I wanted and needed to fly before, but I couldn't. Instead of asking Squire more about that, I decided to tell him about something more important.

"I can make fire now."

He bobbed up and down, as if nodding his approval.

"This morning, I set André's handkerchief on fire and nearly burned him up in his suit. But afterward, I felt… wrong. I felt bad. *The magic* felt bad, like a dark shadow was lurking near me. So now I'm afraid to use my magic."

Squire wrote for a long time. I tried to read it, but couldn't see past his knobby knuckles. Finally, he turned the paper towards me.

"Using magic in anger, or for vengeance, will invite the darkness into your soul. This is black magic, and it will consume you until there is nothing left but that shadow. It's like a virus that feeds on your negative energy. It isn't conscious but it's alive. As a witch, you will always float between the darkness and the light. Only your thoughts and your actions will determine whether you bring in the shadows or the light of love and grace."

"But how do I do that? I mean, what you said — bring in the light of love and grace?" A hard knot tightened in my stomach. I didn't want to be consumed by a shadow; I liked myself the just way I was now.

Squire scribbled again.

"Use magic only to help others. If you cause no harm, the shadow cannot take you. You are only vulnerable if you give into the darkness itself. Do you understand?"

I thought about that for a minute. It wasn't always easy not to cause harm. What if I hurt someone by accident or in self-defense? I remembered the dangerous roughness in my voice after I'd blasted the guard dogs at Irvigne Manor. I was only trying to escape, but I had scared and maybe hurt the poor dogs doing their job. On the other hand, had I not done it, they'd have hurt Jean-Sébastien and me.

The line between good and evil didn't seem so clear.

"What if I hurt someone while helping someone else?" I asked. "Can the darkness still find me then?"

Squire spread his fingers in a shrug and wrote, *"I don't know, so it's best to make sure your intentions are pure."*

That made sense, but it didn't answer my question.

I sat there, contemplating everything Squire had just told me. There was a lot to think about, but I didn't want to talk about the shadows anymore. I wanted to ask Squire more about flying.

"Squire, you said I could fly if I wanted and needed to, right?"

He bobbed up and down in a nod.

"Well, I do want to, and I definitely need to if I'm going to get out of here. But I can't. For one thing, there's no broom in here."

Squire scribbled on the paper and held it up: *"Not all witches fly on brooms."*

"What do they fly on? You mean they can just soar through the air?"

"No. They use whatever they have available. They put their intent into the object and use it to fly."

"Any object?" That seemed incredible. Except, I remembered the old witch in my mother's picture. When she came to life, she flew in a bowl. I was just about to ask Squire about this, when he held up one finger signaling for me to wait. Then he started scribbling. After a couple of minutes, he held up what he'd written.

"*Yes, any object. But, Anna, you should know that once a witch bestows an object with flying power, she must use that type of object forever. Nothing else will ever grant her the ability to fly. When it's time, Anna Sophia, choose carefully.*"

Wow. I looked around the room. There weren't a lot of choices available to me. I didn't want to pick something I'd never see again, like the broken chair I was sitting on, or the disgusting mattress. I would really need to think about it.

"Okay, I will choose carefully. Thanks for explaining it to me."

He bent his knuckles in a bow, as if to say, "you're welcome."

I smiled and asked my next question. "So, I have something else to ask you, okay?"

He nodded.

"The witch in the picture my mother gave me… um, she flew in a bowl."

Squire picked up the stubby pencil and started writing. "*That's your grandmother.*"

"That's my *grandmother?*" I was dismayed. How could that profoundly terrifying person share my blood? The thought of the witch in the picture being my grandmother shocked me so much, all I could think to ask was, "Well, why does she fly in a *bowl*?"

"Actually, it's her enchanted mortar. She uses it to fly, and often will carry her pestle like a club."

Well, that was weird.

"Why doesn't she just fly on her broom? I saw her with a broom in the picture. She used it to sweep off the roof." *The roof of a hut on chicken legs,* I thought to myself as I grimaced.

Squire wrote, "*Yes, she has a broom, but the first time she needed to fly, a broom wasn't available.*"

"So now it can't work for her as a flying instrument, right?"

He nodded.

"Can I ask you another question? It's kind of important."

Squire stopped floating and stayed still in front of me.

"Does she — my grandmother — does she practice black magic?"

Squire hesitated before picking up the pencil. *"Yes,"* he wrote. *"She does. I'm sorry, Anna. It's terrible. She allowed the shadow to take over her soul a long time ago."*

"Who *is* she, Squire? Who is this person you call my grandmother?" I felt the most terrible sense of despair. *Am I doomed? Is it in my blood to bring in the darkness?* I couldn't stop wondering if a terrible fate lay ahead of me simply because I had been born into this family.

If disembodied hands could sigh, Squire probably would have sighed at that moment. Then he wrote. He hovered over the paper for a second, as if unsure if he wanted to show it to me. Finally, he picked it up and turned it so I could see his words.

"*Your grandmother is the Iron Queen. She is infamous in many ways; some good, some bad. Mostly, she scares me. I think she has Knight hidden somewhere.*"

Chapter 31

Dear Diary,

I'm writing this using the paper and pencil stub I found for Squire. I'm glad I can write to you on paper this time, and not just talk to you in my head. Somehow it helps more when I write my thoughts and feelings on paper. Right now, I feel so distraught that I really need to do this.

Squire says my grandmother is called the Iron Queen. He also said she has let the darkness take over her soul. I have no doubt it's true, because she's the witch in the picture, and she scared me half to death. She looked like she had a heart full of shadows and darkness. So, of course, he was telling me the truth. Squire even thinks she is hiding his other hand somewhere. How awful is that? I feel so terrible for him.

Why is there so much darkness in the world? I don't understand.

This is all so unreal. First, I didn't think I had any family at all. Then, I found out I had a living grandmother, and I was so happy. Only now, I find out she is evil. I don't want that woman to be my grandmother! I want someone like Aunt Bea on the old Andy Griffith reruns the Sisters had shown us. I want someone like Sister Daphne. I don't want someone called the Iron Queen — a witch with a soul full of darkness — to be my one living relative.

I wonder why she's called that, anyway. I'll have to ask Squire. But not now, because if I don't get out of here soon, it won't matter that I have a living grandmother. I'll be dead.

My first step is to find something I can fly on. Or fly in. And it has to be something I'll have access to forever, because once I've chosen it, that's it!

I have no idea what will work, but I'll find something.

Wish me luck, Diary!

I spent the next few hours going through the entire room with a fine-toothed comb. I looked at everything with a new eye. My evil grandmother turned a traditional mortar and pestle into her flying machine. I assumed this meant, with the right intent, I could make anything work as my vehicle for flying. But like Squire had said, I needed to be careful about what I chose.

Around noon, Ouellette opened the door. He put a tray of food on the floor, and shoved it inside the room with his toe.

"*Bon appétit*," he said with a smirk.

The tray held a small bowl of porridge, a pitcher of water — no cup or glass — and a withered apple. Quite different from the extravagant buffet Marie had laid out for the party last week.

Last week? It seemed a lifetime ago.

I sighed and forced myself to eat. I wasn't hungry, but I thought I might need the energy later.

By mid-afternoon, I had laid out an assortment of things on the crooked desk: a needle, a spool of red thread, a letter opener, three twist ties, a handful of thumbtacks, a zippered plastic bag, a fork, two pencils, and a stack of paper.

Not much to work with.

I stared at this collection of random objects, and a plan started to come together in my head. It wasn't a great plan. Too many things could go wrong. But my other choice was to wait for the Black Horseman, and that seemed a much worse idea.

Earlier, after I'd found the pencils and the letter opener, I scribbled a note to Jean-Sébastien on a piece of paper. I needed people to know I wasn't dead, and that I had been taken captive. I told him I was in the tower, and as far as I knew, everyone else was still in the dungeon. I warned him about Constable Barnabé being a fake, and Constable Ouellette being real, but dangerous and crooked.

When I gave the paper to Squire, I said, "You need to take this to my friend, Jean-Sébastien. Do you remember him?"

Nod.

"Good. Let's get this window open. Then take it to him as fast as you can."

The window had a bunch of rusty nails keeping it shut, but we used the letter opener to pry them out. The opener got partially shredded in the process, but it was okay because we got the window open.

"Squire," I said, looking at him seriously. "You need to be careful. It's still daylight. Try to fly in the woods whenever you can, ok?"

He nodded, and I had the biggest urge to hug him, except it's kind of hard to hug a floating hand. He must have felt the same way, though, because he dove in and tickled me. I knew that was his way of showing affection.

Chuckling, I said, "Okay, go. And don't be hurt if Jean-Sébastien freaks out a little bit at first. He's never seen anyone quite like you."

Squire nodded, and with a little bow, he turned and flew out the window.

Once he was gone, I felt especially lonely. It seemed so quiet without him. But that was probably good because it meant I had no distractions. I finished searching the room, gathered the few items I wanted to take with me and put them in the plastic bag. I stuffed the bag into the pocket of my robe. I could have used something sturdier than slippers, but there was nothing I could do about that. I couldn't believe I was going to have my first flying experience wearing a ratty old bathrobe and slippers. *Oh, well.*

Truthfully, if I succeeded in flying, I could be dressed in a monkey suit, and I wouldn't care.

I thought a lot about what to choose, and the bucket seemed the only reasonable option. I also wanted to use the mop because it made me feel more secure to hold on to something. I just wasn't sure if it would mean, in the future, I'd only be able to fly if I had both. I wished Squire had still been to tell me these things, but he wasn't.

The bucket was an old metal thing. It was just wide enough for to me to put both feet in it and sit on the edge. It helped to lean on the mop for balance, but I decided it was only the bucket I would concentrate on infusing with flying magic. The mop, if I used it at all, would just serve to help steady me.

Squire had helped me to understand I didn't need to say things like *abracadabra* to make the bucket fly. If it was going to work, it would happen because the magic had come from within me.

I knew I had made the paper torch light up without any feelings of rage or frustration driving the magic, but infusing a bucket with the ability to fly required a lot more power than creating a little bit of fire. I just hoped I could do it.

I closed my eyes and concentrated on breathing. I inhaled slowly and deeply, then exhaled and repeated this several times. Each breath seemed to take me deeper inside myself. Before long, I felt the familiar hum of energy and found myself standing in the midst of a radiating light. It filled me with warmth. I scooped up some of it and formed it into a ball I could hold in my hands. It was so beautiful. I just wanted to hold it so I could stare into it.

Silver, purple, and gold light pulsated around a crystalline blue center. As I stood there, holding the light and being surrounded by it, I experienced the most peaceful feeling I'd ever known.

Surely, there could be no evil in this, I thought. And in that very same instant, I had a flash of awareness. I understood what Squire had tried to explain earlier.

The magic inside me was neither good nor bad. It was pure energy. What determined if it was loving and light, or evil and dark, was me. It was my intent, and how I used it. If I could keep myself from wanting my magic to hurt someone — like André or Ouellette, or anyone else — then the darkness would never have a hold on me.

I understood this perfectly as I stood surrounded by the warm, glowing light.

The question was, could I honor it?

Chapter 32

I thought it might be best to practice flying before leaving the tower. It didn't seem like a good idea to try it for the first time by flying right out the window.

I stepped into the bucket and closed my eyes. As I continued to breathe deeply, I pictured the beautiful blue light as it seeped out of the pit of my stomach and circled me from my head right down to my toes. I watched as it swirled around the bucket, spreading its light inside and out. I pictured myself hovering in the air like Squire, and I felt the bucket begin to shake. With a rough lurch, it lifted off the ground!

The unexpected sensation of floating scared me, and I gasped, which caused the bucket to slam to the floor with a loud thud.

Whoa.

Well, at least I knew it worked. Now I just needed to not freak out when it happened again.

I practiced for another thirty minutes or so. By the time I finished, I wouldn't say I felt confident, but I wasn't gasping in fear anymore. I would have liked to practice longer, but I knew I needed to leave and put my plan in motion before the Black Horseman showed his face again.

I opened the window and felt the wind ruffle my hair. Suddenly, the thought of being so high in the air, in a bucket, had my heart thumping a million beats a minute. I decided to take one more practice run inside.

I zipped clockwise around the room, and for a moment I felt so confident; I was ready to fly out the window. But then a thought crossed my mind: If I plummeted from the sky, I'd surely die a horrible and gruesome death. The instant I had this thought, an interesting thing happened: I crashed.

It was weird. As soon the picture of a wild and uncontrolled dive to earth in a bucket came into my mind, I crashed to the floor with a bang that sent me sprawling across the room.

How odd. Does something happen as soon as I think of it? If so, I better make sure I don't have those kinds of thoughts once I'm really flying!

I stood quietly, wondering if anyone had heard the noise of my crash, but it appeared nobody had. I looked out the window and knew it was time. The sun had set.

I stood in the middle of the room and took one long, deep breath. I could feel the beautiful, blue ball of energy inside me, sparkling with all its threads of silver, gold, and purple. I willed the bucket to rise, and when it did, I hovered for a moment in front of the window. Then, with my eyes wide open, in one decisive swerve, I flew out the window and into the night sky.

A billion stars, just beginning to twinkle, surrounded me. I looked up and saw the moon. I could have sworn she'd winked at me, but when I looked again, she was just there, shining her light upon the earth.

I was flying! Truly flying!

Irvigne Manor was quiet, like a sleeping giant. Lights brightened only a few windows. I floated over the rear garden and toward the labyrinth. It seemed like a logical place to land, so I did, although not very well. When I willed myself downward, I hit the ground with a dull thud, bounced once, and was then ungracefully dumped out of the bucket when it overturned. I wasn't hurt, so it was fine. I figured I'd have plenty of time in the future to practice. At least I hoped I would — that clearly depended on not getting caught while rescuing Mei, Gaëlle, and the rest of the girls.

I grabbed my mop and bucket, and walked into the labyrinth. I took the red thread out of the plastic baggie, which fortunately was still in my pocket. Starting with the first hedge, I tied one end of the red thread to some of its twigs. As I hurried through the maze, the thread trailed behind me. The mop and bucket were awkward to carry and kept bumping my shins, but I didn't dare leave them behind. I just kept going.

I reached the building without error, thanks to the dream stone which thumped against my chest each time I started to take a wrong turn. Looking behind me, I saw the thin thread of red marking the route. *Good. Stage one complete.*

There was no way I could take the mop and bucket through the iron door. Not only might it make it difficult to get in, but I knew I had to quickly and quietly get through the tunnel and to the prison room. I stashed them behind a hedge, where I hoped nobody would notice them if they were in the maze.

It was time to go through the door.

I took a deep breath and closed my eyes. I couldn't believe how easy it was — one second I was standing in the night air, and the next I was sprawled on top of the stone floor.

The pitch-black darkness was a bad as I remembered it. Actually, it was worse because this time I didn't have a candle or Jean-Sébastien with me. I could probably have conjured up a series of magical flames, but I was in no state of mind to figure out how. It didn't matter, though. I needed to move through the tunnel.

I stood up and held both hands in front me, hoping there were no obstacles in the way. Fortunately, there was nowhere to take a wrong turn. I knew if I kept moving as the tunnel sloped downward, I would get to the girls.

I slammed into the second iron door, which I had completely forgotten about. Using my hands to feel my way across it, I came to its edge. I sucked in all my breath, and made it around the door to the other side. I knew then I wasn't far from the dungeon room.

When I saw the faint light, I knew I had reached the end. Within seconds, I was standing at the entrance to the big room. Turning to the right, I walked over to Mei's cell and called to her softly.

I heard her shuffling toward me before she peered through the bars. Hope lit her eyes. "You're back!" she said, her voice filled with relief.

"I am, but we don't have much time," I said. "Can you quietly wake everyone up? I'm going to get the keys to the cells."

Mei nodded.

"Just make sure everyone stays super quiet, Mei, okay? As soon as I have the keys, I'll be back, and we'll all leave."

Both gratitude and fear registered on Mei's face. "Be careful, Anna."

I nodded and moved toward the stairs. I hoped she could quietly shout across the room. If she could wake one person up, that person could wake up the one in the next cell, who could wake the next, until everyone was awake and ready. I didn't know if anyone was in the other two cells with doors — I guessed I would find out once I had the keys.

The guardroom, halfway up the stairs, was dark except for a single candle flickering on the table. Just like when Jean-Sébastien had seen him, the guard was sound asleep and snoring.

I stared at him. He was a big man. Really big. His head was on the table, and his snores made the candle flicker. A single large skeleton key hung from a loop on his belt.

This was the first worrisome part of my plan. I needed to get that key off his belt without waking him up. *But how?* Freezing time didn't seem a reliable skill; the time could start moving again at any moment. I knew I could use my magic to knock the guard out, but I also knew I would then be vulnerable to those terrible shadows. I didn't ever want to be like my grandmother, the Iron Queen. She succumbed, and I vowed I wouldn't — even though this guard *was* responsible for holding everyone captive in those cells. Still, I wasn't about to invite the darkness in just to get even with him for hurting my friends. I had to think of another way.

That was when an idea came to me.

I remembered falling right after I'd imagined myself plummeting from the sky in the bucket. It was, I knew, an important lesson for me, although I just wasn't sure why at the time. But what if I pictured myself completely invisible?

It was worth a try because I sure didn't have any other ideas.

I closed my eyes and pictured energy flowing out of me. In my mind's eye, I saw long golden and silver threads float out of the pit of my stomach and coil around my feet. These beautiful gossamer filaments moved over every part of me, whirling and swirling until they had covered every inch of me from my toes to my head and back to my toes. It felt like a thousand little fairies were covering me in their magic dust.

When there didn't seem to be any more movement, I held my hand out. I couldn't see it! The only discomfort was the growing itch in the middle of my stomach, just above my belly button.

The problem was, I wasn't sure if I was the only one who couldn't see me, or if I would also be invisible to the guard.

There was only one way to know.

Quietly, I stepped into the room and walked until I stood right next to him. I reached for the key on his belt. It was on a mountain climber's carabiner, which was good. It meant all I had to do was open the clip and the key would slip right off.

As I leaned forward to unclip the carabiner, my hair accidentally brushed against the guard's face. He rubbed his face, and I froze. I saw him open one unfocused eye and lazily look around for whatever had tickled his nose. Seeing nothing, he fell back to snoring.

He couldn't see me!

I backed out of the room, and I didn't exhale until I was down the steps and standing outside the prison. By that time, the itch in my stomach was almost too much to bear, so I released the magic, becoming visible again. There was no point in frightening the children even more, anyway.

Wow, I thought. *That worked great! I'm getting better at using my magic.* I just hoped the rest of my plan worked as well.

I walked back into the prison room and went to open Mei's cell first. Thinking the other two cells with doors were empty, I then went across to the six cells side by side. One by one, I unlocked the doors. When I got to the last one, I called Olivia's name. She looked at me blankly before it registered that she knew me. I couldn't believe how much weaker she seemed than just a week ago. I helped her walk over to Mei, who had gathered the other six scraggly-looking children around her.

It surprised me to see three boys among them.

Chapter 33

"Is this everyone?" I asked Mei. She shook her head sadly and nodded toward the cell next to hers. My heart thudded in my chest as I walked over and put the key in the lock. There was only one person who could be in there.

The cell had to be empty because nobody shuffled toward the sound of the turning lock. With relief, I thought Mei must be mistaken — but when I opened the door, I saw why.

"*Gaëlle!*" I screamed in horror as I ran to her. A chain bound her to the wall.

As soon as I reached her, I saw a new bruise darkening one side of her face. I also saw a metal bracelet wrapped around her ankle. It locked onto the chain holding her to the wall of the cell.

"Oh, Gaëlle," I whispered, and the shock of seeing her like this made me want to cry with sorrow. "Did *André* do this to you?"

"No." She shook her head and sniffled. "Marie did. It's my punishment for telling Beatrice the truth about being adopted by them."

"You told her?" I said in surprise. "Gaëlle, that was so brave!" I meant it. It took true courage to stand up to Marie and André by telling Beatrice the truth.

"It didn't matter. She didn't believe me, and then, after we dropped her off at the orphanage, Marie snatched another kid right off the street. He's right over there." Gaëlle pointed toward one of the boys standing next to Mei.

Marie must have been desperate to have all nine kids tonight, I thought. *We have got to get out of here. Fast!*

I tried fitting the key into the lock on Gaëlle's ankle, but it was too big.

"It's no use," said Gaëlle. "You have to leave me. Get the others out of here before it's too late."

"No. You're going, too. Just hold on — I'll be right back."

I told Mei to stay put for a minute, and I ran back up the steps to the guard station. Standing outside his door, and hoping it would work a second time, I went through the process of making myself invisible again. This time I did it faster. I stepped into the room, barely glancing at the snoring man, and grabbed the candle off his table. I prayed the sudden darkness, once I left, wouldn't wake him up.

I raced back to Mei, careful to make sure the flame didn't go out. I started to walk into the room and realized the candle looked like it was floating, since I forgot to make myself visible again. Fortunately, nobody else had seen it.

I walked over to Mei and handed her the candle. "Take this and go the way I came in. You'll follow a long tunnel and then come to an iron door. It's very hard to open, but if a few of you work together, it will turn to the right and open. You'll be in the center of the labyrinth, but don't let it intimidate you. I left a trail of red thread, so you'll be able to find your way out. Just follow it. But you have to hurry, Mei. I don't think we have much time."

She hesitated.

"Go!" I said. "We'll be right behind you. I promise."

Mei nodded and led her little group away. I prayed they would be safe as I hurried back to Gaëlle.

The one hanging bulb in the big room didn't send much light into her cell. Still, I had to find a way to get her unchained from the wall. I fumbled in my pocket for the half-destroyed letter opener.

"I'm going to try opening the lock with this," I said, showing it to her. "Hold your ankle steady."

No matter how much I wiggled it inside the lock, it didn't click open. I tried fitting the sharp edge of the opener through the chain's links, hoping to break it apart. After several tries, the letter opener snapped in half.

Gaëlle whimpered in the dark. "Just go," she said. "You have to help the others."

Sitting back, I raised a hand to calm her. "Shhh. Just wait. Let me think a second."

I knew I could open the lock. It would mean drawing on the red-hot energy I'd used on André in the car, and that was when I first felt the shadow lurking around me. It scared me to call it up again, but I couldn't think of any other way to save Gaëlle. I reminded myself I wasn't using it to harm anyone this time; I was using it to save someone's life.

I couldn't be afraid to use my magic, or it might not work. Squire told me to always have a pure intent because then the darkness had no way to enter. I knew my intent was pure. I needed to trust both myself and the magical energy.

I raised my head to look at Gaëlle. "Listen to me, okay? You're going to feel a little heat, and I hope it doesn't hurt you. Whatever happens, please try not to yell out. No matter what. Okay?" It was a lot to ask of her, I knew. But we couldn't risk waking up the guard.

She nodded, looking genuinely scared.

I closed my eyes and breathed deeply. "Are you ready?" I asked, and I heard her whimper a quiet "yes."

I visualized André's leering face in the car and Ouellette dragging me up the tower steps with my hands cuffed behind my back. The familiar feeling of rage began to build inside my stomach. I thought of Mei and Olivia, pale and thin and locked in filthy prison cells, and I felt the anger grow. I thought of Gaëlle, once so funny and vibrant — and now chained up like a prisoner in the sixteenth century. The intensity of my rage turned into a red, seething fury.

"Close your eyes!" I whispered to Gaëlle. I released a portion of what I tapped into and directed it to the lock on the metal bracelet.

Gaëlle threw her hand over her mouth to muffle her cry of pain. "Ohh! It hurts!" she muttered, and I saw tears fill her eyes.

The bracelet and lock fell to the stone floor with a loud clang.

Not waiting to see if we'd awakened the guard, I grabbed Gaëlle's hand and pulled her out of the cell. I heard the scraping of a chair followed by heavy footsteps on the stairs.

"Run!" I whispered, pushing her toward the rear of the room. Gaëlle groaned, and I realized I must have burned her while removing the lock. I hoped I hadn't hurt her badly because we had a long tunnel to run through in the pitch-black darkness.

I didn't have time to explain where we were going. I said, "Just trust me." I felt her limping beside me as we ran side by side, clutching one another's hand down the black tunnel. Our only relief came at the same time we heard the guard yell, "Hey!" He was carrying a lantern that threw light in front of us.

The hallway grew steeper as we ran upward. My only hope was that the guard was too fat to fit around the iron door in the middle of the tunnel. When we reached it, Gaëlle had no trouble squeezing through the opening because she was so thin.

"Stop!" the guard yelled.

Directly ahead of us, we saw the iron door leading into the labyrinth. It was wide open. I noticed the guard's pounding footsteps had stopped and thought he probably couldn't get past the narrow doorway. Then I heard a loud grunt and the screech of rusty metal. He was strong enough to push it open!

We sprinted toward the exit door and flew through it into the cool night air. I turned and saw the guard's angry face, only steps away.

I hated to use magic in front of Gaëlle; she was traumatized enough by everything she'd experienced. I stopped, feeling red-hot magic in my fingertips, and shot a heavy blast of it at the door, causing it to swing shut with a loud bang, smashing into the guard at the same time.

His yell was muffled by the door, but it still sounded pained. I waited a long moment to see if he would follow us, but the night was silent.

My stomach tightened into knots. I hadn't meant to hurt the guard, only to shut the door and slow him down. But his silence suggested that I had knocked him out. I groaned, releasing the pent-up tension in my belly. Just as I had expected, the emptiness inside me grew, making me feel sick.

Every time I used my magic, I walked a fine line between good and evil. I knew it wouldn't take much effort to push me over to the shadow side. I waited for the darkness to seep away from me again, and soon enough it did, leaving a chunk of it behind in my heart. Although my intentions had been good enough, I hadn't managed to dodge it this time.

Gaëlle hadn't seemed to notice any of this. She was bent over, gasping for breath after our run.

"Let me see your foot," I said.

Without saying a word, Gaëlle raised her foot for me to see. I held her leg, and in the moonlight, I could see a light burn on the surface of her ankle. It killed me to know I had hurt her. I blew on the wound gently, and silently wished it a speedy recovery. Maybe my magic could heal as well as harm.

"We have to find the others," I said.

Gaëlle nodded and stood up, still gasping for breath. She looked so weak. Why hadn't I acted sooner to rescue her from these terrible people who'd starved and tormented her? I wondered if I would ever forgive myself for waiting too long.

"Follow the red thread to get out," I told her. "It will take you to where Mei and the rest of the kids are waiting." I grabbed my mop and pail from where I had hidden it beneath a hedge.

"What about you?" Gaëlle asked.

"You'll see," I said with a shrug. "I'll meet you outside the maze." There was no use trying to hide my secret. By now, Squire had hopefully found Jean-Sébastien. It wasn't like my secret was going to stay one for long.

I hopped into the bucket and closed my eyes, silently calling for my magic. As the bucket rose off the ground, I opened my eyes again, only to see Gaëlle's about ready to pop out of their sockets from shock.

I floated upwards and shouted, "I'll meet you there in a couple of minutes. *Hurry,* Gaëlle!"

As I floated above the hedges, I only hoped Gaëlle's ankle didn't hurt so much she couldn't make it all the way through the labyrinth. I took a moment to breathe deeply and send good thoughts her way. The night air was chilly and crisp, and the moonlight seemed to recharge me. My dream stone hummed on the cord around my neck.

Up ahead, I saw Mei and the others huddled together on the grass, outside the labyrinth. *So far, so good,* I thought. *Stage two successfully completed. One more stage to go.*

My good feelings lasted until I landed in the grass and André stepped out of the garden with Marie.

"Don't think you'll get away that easily," he said, gazing at me with an easy smile. "You and those filthy kids aren't going anywhere." With a nasty sneer, he leaned forward and whispered, "Gotcha, little witch."

Chapter 34

André looked at me with such a satisfied grin on his face, I had to use all my self-control not to send so much fire his way that he'd need the entire fire department to put it out. I knew now why the dream stone had shown me the evil that was suffocating every living thing at Irvigne Manor. The evil lived inside André and Marie. It oozed out their pores like sweat and destroyed everything in their path.

Well, no more!

I felt all the magic roiling inside me and churning with a frenzy I hadn't felt before. Before I could do a thing though, I heard a loud clicking sound and suddenly floodlights saturated the entire property. It became so bright, it might as well have been daytime.

André laughed. "I love modern conveniences — don't you, Anna Sophia?" His face turned dark. "Makes it hard to sneak out of here, doesn't it? In fact, I'd say, it makes it *impossible* to sneak out of here." He chuckled and turned to Marie. "What do you think, darling?"

"Yes. Simply impossible." She smiled at me sweetly, but her eyes were cold enough to freeze the Sahara Desert.

All the children stood huddled together, close enough to hear André's chilling words. They clutched at one another with looks of sheer terror. Their faces said it all: It was worse almost escaping and getting caught than just having stayed in their cells. At least there, they knew what to expect.

There were five girls and three boys. Gaëlle and I made ten. There was one extra, since Marie didn't think I'd be there when she snatched the last boy after dropping off Beatrice at the orphanage.

All of a sudden, Gaëlle stepped out of the maze — and froze.

"Ah, Gaëlle," Marie said. "*So* good of you to join us, dear. How wonderful! Now, the whole gang is here."

"You won't get away with this, *Mother,*" Gaëlle said. I was glad to see some of her old spunk had risen to the occasion. It gave me hope she would bounce back from this ordeal, once it was all over.

"Oh, child. Don't be so dramatic," Marie said. "We already have gotten away with it. They all think Anna killed Mei. As to her — well, everyone thinks your friend Anna Sophia died in a horrific car accident. Poor child. May she rest in peace. You'll be staying at our house in Scotland. And the rest of these brats are nothing but guttersnipes. No one will miss them. So, you see, darling: We really have gotten away with it."

I winced at her words. Every child should be loved enough to be missed by someone, and no child should be written off as a "guttersnipe." Her words seemed to inspire a new kind of rage in me. Instead of the familiar red-hot anger, this felt like pure, ice-cold fury.

I looked around and thought, *this is not over yet. I haven't worked this hard and pushed my magic to its limits for this to end here.*

But for now, all I could do was stall for time and hope that Jean-Sébastien had gotten someone to believe him and was on his way with help. My hand slipped into my pocket and started to fiddle with the plastic bag.

"Why are you doing this?" I asked. "Why do you steal children? Does it make you feel powerful?"

"Don't be stupid," Marie said. "Only money is power. And we do this for the money. Do you think keeping up a castle is cheap? We have standards to uphold, you know." She smiled sarcastically and held her hand out to admire her fingernails.

I kept fiddling with the bag. I was trying to pry it open without André and Marie noticing any movement in my pocket.

"Well, all I can say is thank you," I said.

I saw everyone turn to look at me in surprise. Of course, Marie's overly tweezed eyebrows didn't allow her to express much of anything. Still, I sensed her shock.

"That's right," I said, looking at her. "You've instilled a lot of strength and courage in all of us that we didn't even know we had. That's a good thing." I silently thanked Malala for being my inspiration.

I just needed to stall them a little longer now.

"What a ridiculous child." André boomed. "Enough of your foolishness. *Ouellette!*"

Ouellette stepped from behind the cluster of trees where he must have been watching and listening to our exchange.

Coward.

"Take our *darling children* back to their cells," André commanded. "And make sure they stay there this time." His voice carried an unspoken but harsh threat.

My hand finally grasped the thumbtacks inside the baggie, and I scooped them out. Sending a shot of magic through my fingers into the tacks, I released them into the air just as Ouellette grabbed Mei's arm. The tacks flew at him like angry bees. One after another, their needle-sharp points pricked Ouellette repeatedly, covering his stomach, face, and neck.

Ouellette yelled as he tried to block his face from the onslaught of tacks. Mei stomped on his foot and ran, pushing the other children ahead of her. Ouellette stumbled blindly, shrieking and swatting at his face as the tacks continued their assault. He tripped over something and fell face-first on the gravel path. He didn't get back up.

"Why you little... *witch*!" André snarled, as if he couldn't think of anything else to call me. He grabbed my arm, but I shot my magic deep into the ground, anchoring my feet. I badly wanted to hurt him. But after I'd hurt Gaëlle, the guard, and Ouellette, the darkness of black magic had been spreading around me fast already. I did want to hurt André. But I wanted to save my soul more.

I used my magic to resist him rather than to hurt him. "You will not take any of us," I said stubbornly. "You don't get to steal us."

He yanked at me, but my feet had firmly anchored themselves to the ground.

"Your stupid magic won't help you," he said through clenched teeth. "I'll cut off your feet and sell you to the Black Horseman in pieces if I have to." He was so angry he was spitting as he threw his ugly words at me. "I'll still get top dollar for your scrawny little body. The Horseman tells me your grandmother will pay handsomely to get you back. She could care less in what condition."

My grandmother? This all has something to do with my grandmother?

My heart sank to my knees. "You're lying!" But even as I said those words, I could feel he was telling the truth. *The Black Horseman works for my grandmother*, I thought, and a horrible wave of nausea washed over me. *That's why he's so interested in me.*

Was all of this my fault?

I wondered if all these kids were being sent to my grandmother for some reason. And, if so, did it have something to do with me?

It was a thought too horrible for me to bear, and for the first time, I understood why my mother had hidden me in Mama Bear's den. She was keeping me away from the Iron Queen — keeping me from her own mother.

André's voice startled me and brought my attention back to what was happening in front of me.

"I have a brilliant idea!" he said, clapping his hands gleefully. "Marie! How about you start gutting the children so Anna Sophia can see the price of her stubbornness! What a glorious idea! Let's start with her pretty friend, Gaëlle."

"Darling, you *are* brilliant." Pulling a huge butcher's knife from her purse, Marie rushed to Gaëlle and grabbed her by the arm. I saw Gaëlle's entire body begin to shake with sobs.

I no longer cared if the darkness consumed my soul. I would not let them hurt Gaëlle! More angry magic swirled inside me than I had ever felt before. Just as I was about to gather it up, a large stone flew out of the darkness and hit Marie in the chest.

She jerked back with a sharp *"Oomph!"* and dropped her knife.

Gaëlle kicked Marie's leg and pushed her away. As she ran toward me, more and more stones flew out of the shadows. I heard a familiar voice yell, "Get them!"

Jean-Sébastien!

Jean-Sébastien, Luca, the Sisters, and all the kids from my floor burst out from behind the bushes. Some continued to lob stones at André and Marie, while Sister Constance gripped her cane and waved it in the air in front of her like she was bushwhacking her way through a jungle. Sister Daphne, right behind Sister Constance, waved a rolling pin over her head as if it were a sword. Squire bobbed alongside them carrying a baseball bat.

André and Marie yelled in alarm and ran. They were bigger cowards than Ouellette, who I noticed was no longer laying on the ground. *Where did he go?*

As soon as they caught sight of the kidnapped kids, Sister Daphne dropped her rolling pin and ran toward them. Immediately, she was hugging all the children who surrounded her. Even the ones who didn't live in the orphanage clutched for her wherever they could find a spare arm or leg. Those who couldn't find a place to nestle close to Sister Daphne found comfort in the arms of Sister Constance. It warmed my heart to see it.

Kicking off my slippers which had become a soggy, muddy mess, I ran after the Montmorencys. I felt strangely vulnerable, running barefoot in my bathrobe, but I wasn't going to let it slow me down.

"They went around the hedge," Jean-Sébastien yelled, following right on my heels. We rounded the corner of the maze and saw the couple halfway to the clearing. If they got much farther, they'd disappear into the forest, where we might never find them.

I stopped in my tracks and took a deep breath as I gathered up every bit of magic I felt inside me.

Jean-Sébastien slammed into me from behind, and we both nearly tumbled to the ground. We probably would have, if I hadn't been standing there like a silent monolith, forming my energy into a cobalt-blue ball. He took one look at my face and silently backed up. He knew exactly what I was doing. He'd seen it before.

Darkness and shadows flitted around the edge of my vision. I didn't care. The rage growing in my chest was filling up every bit of me. With one last deep breath, I let the magic blast from my hands in one long stream of cold, blue power. Immediately, red-hot rockets of exploding rage followed. It was like watching a series of grenades detonate in front of our eyes. The power of it all was so great it took my breath away.

I didn't aim any of it directly at André or Marie. Instead, I aimed it at the row of hedges just behind them. When the magic hit, they burst into life. Long, twisted vines uncurled like arms. Powerful, gnarled fingers at the ends of each vine reached for André and Marie. Snatching them up, they held them firmly in place against the hedge wall. More vines coiled around their feet, making it impossible for them to move so much as a hair on their heads.

Marie screamed.

Chapter 35

By the time Jean-Sébastien and I had reached André and Marie, they were captives against the hedges. Marie looked our way with pure hatred in her eyes. She tried to lunge for me, but the vine jerked her backward. She yelped and held still.

"You never do cease to amaze me, Anna," Jean-Sébastien said, struggling for breath. "I didn't think anything could top the dogs, but this did. This most definitely did."

I looked at him in surprise. I had expected that my magic would freak him out, but it didn't. His eyes shone with excitement.

"You remember that 'strange on steroids' thing I said a week or so ago? I take it back. It doesn't begin to cover the kind of strange you are." He laughed. "Not even a little. You're way more awesome than that!"

I blushed at his praise. It surprised me — except, even though I was embarrassed, a kind of a warm glow also filled me. I was happy he thought I was strange in a good way.

By then, everyone else had caught up to us, so I didn't have time to think about Jean-Sébastien anymore. That was probably a good thing. I smiled when Squire dropped the bat he was holding and flew up to my shoulder so he could sit on it. His nearness sent a warm feeling all the way through me.

The shock of the night started to sink in, and even with Squire on my shoulder, I began to feel cold. My stomach buzzed from all the effort, and my chest felt like someone had shot a cannonball through it.

"You brats!" André growled. "You'll all be sorry—"

I stopped his cursing by wrapping another vine around his face. It bit into his mouth like a gag.

"Be quiet!" I snapped. "You have lost the right to speak here."

I was stunned I had spoken so authoritatively to André — but I was still mad, and it just popped out of me. Even so, it didn't stop me from feeling satisfied I had shut him up, both physically and verbally. I didn't know if that feeling would bring in the darkness, and I wasn't about to think it to death. Not right then, anyway.

I turned to look at the others. What a group they were — nearly a dozen half-starved kids in torn clothing, all my friends who had been startled out of their evening routine and had arrived in pajamas, and of course, Sisters Daphne and Constance.

The only one missing was Lauraleigh. At first, I couldn't understand why she hadn't come, until I remembered it was the night her grandfather had arranged to take her out to dinner as a graduation present.

I turned to the Sisters. "What should we do now?" I asked.

Surprisingly, it wasn't they who answered me. It was all the kids around them.

"Kill them!"

"Cut off their faces!"

"Bury 'em!"

"Let them stay there and starve to death!"

I was shocked by what they were saying, but I could hardly blame them. How long had the Montmorencys kept them in that horrible dungeon, alone, cold, and in the dark? Those kids would never get over their experience at Irvigne Manor. Still, none of us should've been thinking about killing or harming others. I didn't think only witches needed to worry about darkness and shadows taking over our souls. I began to think everyone had to worry about that.

"You caught them, Anna," Jean-Sébastien said. "You should decide what to do with them."

I shrank at the thought and turned toward André and Marie. They were bound head to toe in rough vines. Their eyes, bulging with fear, pleaded with me for mercy.

I could feel the emptiness that had already found a home inside me jumping with glee. *"They don't deserve mercy! They deserve everything you can throw at them,"* an angry voice inside of me hissed.

"Remember Mei in the dungeon. Remember the bruises on Gaëlle's face and how they chained her to the wall. Think about how they were going to send all of you to some unknown fate with an evil witch whose heart doesn't even know love. No mercy for them! No mercy!"

The voice pressed on, whispering and pushing at me. I knew it wasn't me talking — it was the shadow. It was the little piece of darkness I had let into my heart when I'd used my magic to hurt people tonight. Even though I did realize this, for some reason, the more I listened to it, the more it made sense. André and Marie had to be stopped. No one would believe us. I'd already gone to the police, and look how that turned out.

Yes, I stood there thinking. *The only one with enough power to stop them is me.*

With that thought, magic surged through my veins. It began to hurt as it coursed through me; it was that powerful. I knew the only way to stop the pain was to release all the energy pulsating against my skin, begging to be free. All I had to do was shoot my magic into that tangle of branches. It would light up like a bonfire, and André and Marie would be gone forever. Never again would they be able to harm another child.

My stomach and fingers tingled with unshed energy. I held up my hands. André's eyes nearly blew out of their sockets. He groaned.

"Do it! Do it!" the shadow whispered. *"Punish them! See how wonderful it will feel."*

But other voices spoke inside me too.

"Ahh-na. No. Ahh-na... you will make yourself no better than them."

"Malyshka, *remember: You can be fearless and gentle at the same time. This is your chance to grow your spirit and strengthen your soul, my dear* Malyshka. *Choose with care."*

"Anna. Be kind even when those around you are not. You will be better for this choice."

They were all there — all talking to me at once. The darkness, Malala, Uncle Misha, and Anne Frank.

It felt like the world was spinning around me, when I finally shouted, "No! I can't." I dropped my hands, gulping down tears of fear and pain.

Magic still coursed through me, demanding to be used. I raised my hands and shot a pure blast of energy into the sky. Then I collapsed, wracked with pain and that awful emptiness from opening myself to the darkness.

Squire floated over to me and laid his fingers on my shoulder again. Only he knew what danger I had truly just faced.

The crowd behind me was silent. Sister Constance picked her way carefully through the jumble of roots and vines, and wrapped her arms around me.

"You did well," she said. "It's not your job to save the world. We'll leave that to the professionals." She tilted her head toward the house. Many people, some wearing police uniforms, were running towards us, led by my beloved Monsieur Nolan.

I smiled and sank into Sister Constance's arms.

"I've heard enough," Monsieur Nolan said after listening to André and Marie's tearful confession for nearly ten minutes. "Haven't you, Commissioner Troy?"

The two criminals were still tangled in the mess of vines, and we all stood in a semicircle in front of them. A gentle wind whispered through the vines. The hedge didn't seem alive anymore. The branches were just like they always had been — except, of course, for still harboring André and Marie.

The Police Commissioner was a tall man with a slight stoop. His long, craggy face was set in a scowl. André and Marie had tried to blame everything on the mysterious Black Horseman, which was convenient since he wasn't there. But several children spoke up about the abuse they'd received at their hands.

"I don't know about any Horseman," one tough little boy said. "But those two grabbed me off my bike. It was in the park in Annecy. I haven't seen my mom and dad since Christmas."

Commissioner Troy looked lovingly at the little boy and hunkered so he could speak with him eye to eye. "I want you to know we have been looking for you all this time. Your parents will think they are seeing an angel when they see you. They've been waiting a long, long time for this night."

He had a tear in his eye as he stood tall again and said, "I believe I've heard enough. Enough for me to make sure they are put away for the rest of their sorry lives. *Take them away.* I can't bear the sight of them for another minute."

Two constables looked at him dubiously. "Uh, sir," one of them said. "How do we get them out of there?"

"Use your brain," the Commissioner said. "Find an ax!"

Just then, we saw two constables dragging a handcuffed Ouellette through the grass. Pinpricks pockmarked his face, and he had snot running out of his nose, giving away the fact that he'd been crying. Not even his magic could save him from the wrath of fellow officers who'd felt betrayed by one of their own.

Commissioner Troy drew himself up to his full height. "Ouellette," he said coldly, nodding at the blubbering man. "You must know that whatever fate awaits the Montmorencys, if it takes until my dying breath, I will make sure yours is a thousand times more painful." Turning to the two constables holding him up, Commissioner Troy waved his hand at them angrily. "Get him out of here. He contaminates the air we're breathing."

I realized something as I looked at Ouellette. There were probably levels of power when it came to magic, just like with everything else. And his level wasn't very high. If it had been, he would have exploded right out of those cuffs, or blown the constables, and all of us, into the vines so we would be held captive. But he didn't do any of that because he couldn't. He was nothing more than an oversized bully who used his little bit of power to scare a thirteen-year-old girl.

As the police dragged Ouellette away, the Commissioner walked up to André and tore away the vine that was covering his mouth again.

"André, I considered you a friend," he said. "We've played cards every Wednesday. You've had dinner with my family. And now I find that you are some kind of a… *monster!*"

"I'm not the monster; she is!" André nodded at me. "She's a witch!"

I rose on wobbly legs and stood right in front of him. "What's the matter, André? You said you could handle one little girl," I taunted.

He narrowed his eyes at me. "You think you're safe now. Well, little witch, let me tell you something. You're *not*." His snarl turned into a vicious grin. "I wouldn't want to be you when your grandmother finally catches up with you, an—"

Before he could say another word, Squire jumped off my shoulder. Balling his hand into a fist, he hit André square in the face. André yelled as blood poured from his nose. I was pretty sure Squire had broken it.

I wondered if disembodied hands had to worry about the darkness.

Chapter 36

While André blubbered about his nose, the two constables went to find an ax.

Commissioner Troy and Monsieur Nolan gathered up the children, right after Monsieur Nolan hugged me for so long I thought he might never let me go. The relief on his face at seeing me unharmed almost made me cry.

The two of them explained they would take everyone who had been held captive at Irvigne Manor to the hospital. There, doctors would examine them before releasing them into the care of the orphanage or their parents. Commissioner Troy said it would be the happiest moment of his long career to call all the parents and let them know their children were safe.

Before returning to the orphanage, Mei and Gaëlle also had to go to the hospital. I imagined both would have to be there for at least a few days. That was okay, because it would give me time to get my room ready to share with Gaëlle again — something that made me very happy.

Sisters Constance and Daphne drove me back to the orphanage in a minibus, along with Jean-Sébastien, Luca, and all the other kids who had come to help. On the way there, Luca turned to me. He said, "How did you do that with the robotic hand? It was so cool. I've never seen tricks like that, except on TV!"

I looked at him in surprise. Before I could say anything, one of the other kids said, "You have all sorts of cool tricks. Like that thing with the vine. Did you have some kind of remote control thing to make them do that? That was *awesome*!"

I glanced at Jean-Sébastien, who just shrugged and smiled. "No sense in telling them everything," he whispered. "A girl ought to have a few secrets, don't you think?"

Are you kidding me?

I had been going over and over and over in my head how I was going to explain to everybody about being a witch. But nobody seemed too concerned about it — either they didn't believe what they'd seen, or they thought I had done some parlor magic. It didn't seem to cross anyone's mind, including the Sisters, that a true supernatural phenomenon had just taken place. I couldn't believe it.

Except for Jean-Sébastien. He knew. He'd seen too much to think any of it was done with a store-bought magic kit. However, for whatever reason, he was good with letting it remain unspoken. There was something very special about that, and I liked knowing we shared such an important secret. I would always be grateful to him for his part in rescuing everyone from Irvigne Manor.

We pulled up to the orphanage, and Lauraleigh came running out, tears streaming down her face.

"Are you all right?" she asked, pulling me into a giant hug the second I got out of the car. "I was out this evening, and when I came back, everyone was gone. The few younger kids here said you'd been kidnapped by André and Marie. I've never felt so scared!" She hugged me so tight I couldn't have possibly gotten enough air to tell her I was fine. But, that was okay; I was sure she knew it on her own.

Later that night, after Lauraleigh and I had spent hours talking, and I had told her nearly the whole story about the Montmorencys, she said, "I knew you had a good reason for hurting your ankle. And I sure knew it wasn't football!"

We laughed a long time over that. When we were done laughing, I told her about the darkness. I told her how afraid I was of something bad inside of me. Something that was alive like a virus, and intent on keeping me from using my magic for good.

"I wish you had been given the power instead of me," I said.

"Me? Why me?"

"Because you're naturally good and kind. You'd never have to worry about letting blackness into your heart the way I do."

Lauraleigh was quiet for a minute. "You're wrong about that, Anna Sophia. I have a dark side."

"You *do*?" Nothing could have surprised me more.

"Everyone does, Anna. Inside all of us are two people waging war every day. One is kind and good and filled with love, joy, and compassion. The other is angry and dark, filled with greed and jealousy, and always seeking revenge."

"Really?" I couldn't imagine any of those dark and angry traits living inside of her.

"Of course, silly!"

"How come I never see the dark and angry person that lives in you? How come only the nice one always comes out?"

"Well, that's simple, Anna." She smiled. "I only feed one of them."

I didn't know what to say. Nothing had ever made more sense to me. I looked at Lauraleigh and grinned. "That's so smart of you."

"I think so," she said, and gave me another big hug.

I had a feeling that as long as Lauraleigh was in my life, along with Monsieur Nolan and Uncle Misha, it would be easier to remember not to feed the darkness inside of me.

I hoped so, anyway.

Afterword

ear Diary,

I've filled nearly a whole notebook with letters to you! I'll have to start a new one soon. Thank you for always listening to me and helping me sort through my thoughts. It's kind of like what Anne Frank says: "I can shake off everything as I write; my sorrows disappear, my courage is reborn." That is very true for me, as well.

Lauraleigh and the other seniors graduated yesterday. They all looked so wise standing there, receiving their diplomas. Especially Lauraleigh. I only hope, one day, I can be as wise as she is now.

I've been nervous after the experiences at Irvigne Manor. I've not been sleeping well because I keep having strange and disconcerting dreams about my grandmother, the Iron Queen. Around every corner, I keep thinking I'll see the Black Horseman with his long, black ponytail and piercing, dark eyes. I keep thinking he is going to kidnap me and take me to my grandmother's, wherever it is she lives.

Candace lives at the orphanage now. I almost feel sorry for her. She's still way too bossy, but now no one pays her any attention.

Little Beatrice isn't talking to me. Somehow, she blames me for losing what she calls "the perfect family." I suspect Candace has been filling her head with lies. I spoke to

Sister Daphne about it, and she promised to keep an eye on Beatrice. I can't do more than that. I know how much Beatrice wanted to find a family, but I'm not sorry that I helped capture the Montmorencys.

They go to trial next week. The evidence against them is overwhelming, and I'm sure they'll go to prison for a very long time. Ouellette, too. I hear that prison isn't a fun place for ex-police officers. Oh, well. He should have thought of that before working for criminals.

The police are also investigating the fates of all those other girls who, according to the Montmorencys, had gone to universities abroad after turning seventeen. There seems to be a profound shock in the city about why no one had ever questioned where those kids went, and why no one had linked the disappearances of so many children to this rich couple.

If it were up to me, I'd also have asked them to investigate why did so many adults ignore how miserable children looked soon after their adoption into the Montmorency family. How could there be such a dramatic failure of child protection? Was everyone so enamored with the couple's wealth and outward charity?

Lauraleigh noticed how jumpy I've been, and when Monsieur Nolan was visiting one evening, she mentioned it to him. We all had a long talk after that. Lauraleigh wants to take a gap year and travel around the world with a backpack. She has grandparents in Tuscany, which is an area in Italy, and she suggested to Monsieur Nolan that we go there together. He thought it was a great idea and said he'd make all the arrangements.

We all decided it would be best not to tell anyone except Sisters Constance and Daphne where I'm going. And Gaëlle, of course, since she's back from the hospital and sharing a room with me again. She won't tell anyone. The only thing I feel bad about is leaving her. She's been quiet, and I know it's hard for her to come to terms with everything that has happened. But she's strong, and the Sisters introduced her to a counselor who can help her move forward and be happy again.

So, that's about it, Diary. Lauraleigh and I leave for Italy in just a few days. I can't wait. I guess the next time I write you, it will be from there!

Thank you for always being here for me. I'm so glad Anne Frank taught me about diaries. And, well, lots of other things, too.

Ci sentiamo presto, Diary! That means "talk to you soon" in Italian. Lauraleigh taught it to me.

Love,
Anna Sophia, teenage girl witch

PS. Uncle Misha was right, as usual. We shouldn't ever be afraid of change.

I dumped my bag in the room down the hall from Lauraleigh's. The flight to Florence had taken longer than we'd expected, with delays at the connecting airport in Zurich. By the time we arrived at her grandparents' villa in the hills outside Pisa, the afternoon sun had splashed the landscape in beautiful, soft yellows.

My room was all done in pastel colors, and I felt like I was sitting in an Old World painting. Lauraleigh's grandmother had been very welcoming when we arrived. She was a big woman with sturdy arms, and when she hugged me, I felt… safe.

We left Luyons in an uproar. The scandal about the lack of attention to the children adopted by the Monmorencys was all over the news, and some activist groups were already demanding changes in the adoption laws. André and Marie had been convicted and sentenced to ninety years in jail. They would never see the light of day again. Ouellette had been convicted too, but on the night before his sentencing, he disappeared from his cell. No one could figure out how he had escaped. It was like… well, like magic.

I shuddered, thinking that both Ouellette and the Black Horseman were out there somewhere. They wouldn't let me get away that easily. But I was safe here in Tuscany. It was all very cloak-and-dagger, but no one would find me here.

Or so I'd thought.

I opened the window to let in the sweet afternoon air, and a crow landed on the sill. I jumped back. The bird cawed and cocked its head, gazing at me with its glistening eye. A small metal tube was fastened to its foot.

Hesitantly, I reached for it. The crow stood still while I opened the tube and took out a small rolled paper. Then it cawed again and flew away.

"What was that?" asked Lauraleigh, who had stepped into the room. Her eyes were wide with surprise.

"It's a note," I said in astonishment. "From Uncle Misha!"

My dear Anna Sophia,

I don't know if you have received my recent letters. I fear you have not. Forces have been working to keep us apart. Our enemies may have intercepted my mail. But I trust dear Bartholomew, my faithful crow, will find you with this letter.

I'm afraid he brings terrible news though. Your father is missing, and I fear he may have been taken by the Red Horseman. Dark spirits watch my every move, and I cannot go to his aid.

I know you have never met your father, and you may feel that he abandoned you. Nothing could be further from the truth. I promise, Malyshka, as soon as I see you, I will explain everything. You must hurry. Meet me at my hut by the new moon, or I fear that it will be too late to save your father.

Trust Monsieur Nolan, but speak of this to no one else. I cannot wait to hold my little Malyshka again.

Your loving Uncle Misha.

The letter floated to the floor. I looked into Lauraleigh's worried eyes.

"I have to leave. Right now."

THE END

Would you like to know what happened next?

Go here: http://www.amazon.com/dp/B01AF1HDDA (AMAZON US) or http://www.amazon.co.uk/dp/B01AF1HDDA (AMAZON UK) to buy Book 2: Wandering Witch

TO SUBSCRIBE - SO YOU CAN LEARN ABOUT VIC CONNOR'S NEW RELEASES AND DISCOUNTS, PLEASE GO HERE: http://bit.ly/Anna_Subscribe

If You Enjoyed this Book...

...I would really, really appreciate if you could help others njoy it, too. Reviews are like gold dust and they help persuade other readers to give the stories a shot. More readers means more incentive for me to write, and that means there'll be more stories, more quickly.

By leaving a review of this book, you can make a difference. And the good news is that it doesn't take long.

You can do it at the book's page here:

http://www. amazon.com/dp/B01A3GQ65I.

Also by Vic Connor

Max! (age 7+)

The year is 1983, and the Cold War between America and the Soviet Union is escalating again. In the small Soviet town of Belsk though, a young Russian teenager has bigger things on his mind, matters much more pressing to a boy in the seventh grade.

Maxim Lapin has a crush. And not just any crush. Maxim is head over heals for a girl named Tanya Nosova, and it's just his luck that Tanya is too ambitious and independent to even acknowledge his advances.

As if that wasn't enough, Maxim and his friends are being bullied by a gang of older boys, led by angry, frightening Tolik Smirnov.

Tommy Hopps and the Aztecs (age 9+)

When he takes a family vacation to Mexico City, Tommy Hopps is just a normal, fourteen-year old kid — but that's all about to change.

Sleeping soundly in his family's hotel room, Tommy is awoken by a ghostly presence: a threadbare, swashbuckling pirate. When the strange intruder attacks his mother and father, Tommy fights back. And that's where the story begins…

Books by Max Candee:

Globaloonies series (age 6+)

Like most boys that age, Joey has a pet chameleon named Larry and a mysterious Big Red Button that can transport the two of them through time and space to the far reaches of the planet...

Hey, wait a second, that's not typical at all! In fact, that's pretty amazing — which is why you'll want to follow along as Joey and Larry set off on their first Big Red Button adventure.

Whatta Weird World series (age 6+)

During the day, Amanda Grace has a bedroom like any other little girl, with a bed and a desk and a shelf where she keeps her favorite books. But during the night, when everyone's asleep, her room transforms into a dream Adventure Castle with butterfly pictures on its pink walls ... and lots of exciting goings-on all around.

About the Author

Vic Connor is a dad of three curious kids. He writes books for middle grade children together with fourteen-year-old son Ivan, who shares his passionate opinions and creative ideas.

In fact, Vic only publishes those books which his son and other children loved and wanted to share with their friends.

For more information:

@TheVicConnor

TheVicConnor

www.MaxedOutKid.com

vic@vicconnor.com

Made in the USA
Middletown, DE
11 August 2018